"This here can, Cadigan, is Bill Lancaster. Kill him."

And Cadigan fired. There was a clang far above. The can was dashed still higher, then fell straight down.

"What's next?" asked Cadigan, as he began to load his revolvers for a fresh attempt.

"You're done," said Loftus. "Cadigan, you're as good a hand with a gun as I ever seen. They ain't no fear in you. A scary gent, he can't have no luck with a gun. I done made a first-class shot outa you."

"Can I start for Lancaster now?" asked Cadigan, grinning with joy.

"They ain't no man in the world that you couldn't start for now," said Uncle Joe gravely.

WARNER PAPERBACK LIBRARY BOOKS

BY MAX BRAND

The Smiling Desperado
Outlaw Breed
The Invisible Outlaw
Silvertip's Strike
Silvertip's Chase
Silvertip
Showdown
Smugglers' Trail
The Granduca
Big Game
The Rescue of Broken Arrow
Border Bandit
Six Golden Angels
The Sheriff Rides
Gunman's Legacy
Valley Vultures
Trouble Trail
Marbleface
The Return of the Rancher
Mountain Riders
Slow Joe
Happy Jack
Brothers on the Trail
The Happy Valley
The King Bird Rides
The Long Chance
The Man From Mustang
Mistral
The Seven of Diamonds
Dead or Alive
Smiling Charlie
Pleasant Jim
The Rancher's Revenge
The Dude
Riders of the Plains
The Jackson Trail
The Iron Trail
Pillar Mountain
The Blue Jay
Silvertip's Search
Silvertip's Trap
Silvertip's Roundup
Outlaw's Code
Montana Rides!
Montana Rides Again
Outlaw Valley
The Song of the Whip
Tenderfoot

MAX BRAND

THE SMILING DESPERADO

A Warner Communications Company

WARNER PAPERBACK LIBRARY EDITION
FIRST PRINTING: MARCH, 1974

LIBRARY OF CONGRESS CATALOG CARD NUMBER: 52-13137

THIS WARNER PAPERBACK LIBRARY EDITION IS PUBLISHED BY ARRANGEMENT WITH DODD, MEAD & CO., INC.

COVER ILLUSTRATION BY CARL HANTMAN

WARNER PAPERBACK LIBRARY IS A DIVISION OF WARNER BOOKS, INC., 75 ROCKEFELLER PLAZA, NEW YORK, N.Y. 10019.

A Warner Communications Company

Printed in the United States of America

Contents

1

DANNY STOPS THE SPEEDING MILL

No one noticed Danny Cadigan until his tenth year. Up to that point he was simply a sleek, good-natured boy with sleepy black eyes and a sluggish body. But in his tenth year, on a brisk windy day in March, the long rope which was used to pull the fan out of the wind and bind it to the side of the wheel, snapped short at its head, dropped its long length upon the head of the school-teacher, and made her squeal with fear.

She clasped her hands together with alarm and ran back from beneath the mill to see what was happening. Of course, the fan snapped out into the gale at once, and the wheel turned into a flashing gray disk, so rapidly did it begin spinning.

That was not all. She had gone to turn the mill off because the tank which supplied the needs of the school—both for the thirsty children and for the horses which they drove or rode for many miles—had been filled to the brim and the drainage pipe which took the overflow from the top of the tanks had been spurting a white stream and turning the ground in front of the entrance to the school into a lake.

The teacher was frantic. That forming pool meant that the children would tramp into the building with muddy feet for days and days to come. It meant wet shoes, it meant colds, it meant sneezes, it meant swollen red noses and dull eyes and duller brains.

And there was already so much work to make up! What would the trustees have to say to her at the end of the spring term? And how could she explain to them that it was all on account of a pool of water in front of the school, caused by the breaking of the rope which—

No mere man could understand these long chains of causes and effect; it required a woman; it required a woman's tact and—er—intuition!

So said Miss Sophie Preston in her bodeful heart as she watched the wheel stagger and moan with speed in the full face of the storm, and as she saw the plunger racing loosely up and down, forcing water out of the seams of the pump at every stroke. The stream rushed into the tank faster than the overflow pipe could accept it. And now a thousand little rivulets began to streak to the side of the tank.

Miss Preston ran hysterically back into the schoolhouse.

"Oh," she cried, clasping her hands, "who can stop the mill—it's running away! The rope is broken!"

The whole roomful of children poured outdoors. There was that in the words and in the manner of the teacher which suggested a picture of the windmill striding away across the landscape with gigantic steps. In a wide semicircle, then, they grouped around the four iron legs of the mill and craned their necks to watch the racing wheel. There was nothing novel about it. Every one of them had seen racing mills before; but the hysteria of the teacher was catching. They began to gape and whisper to one another. Besides, nothing is so confusing, so unnerving, as a wind storm. Above the head of the mill they could see the clouds torn to shreds and hurried across the sky. And when one of the eighth grade boys yelled: "Look at Danny Cadigan!" his voice was a mere whistle above the storm.

Then they saw Danny Cadigan climbing slowly up the

long ladder, his fat little body swaying from side to side in the pressure of the gale. He made no haste. He climbed very leisurely, a step at a time, steadying himself on both

[illegible]

sat in the shade of one of the trees near the schoolhouse, or else he leaned against the corner of the building and blinked his big, lazy black eyes at the others. Even the activity of sport did not greatly appeal to him. He preferred to drowse and dream and watch the others. He was not even bothered by the bullies of the school, for it was taken for granted that such an inactive one would not fight, and would not offer sport even if he was maltreated. He was merely a drone in a busy hive. At some time he would be stung by one of the workers. But up to the present he was too small to be noticed. He was a nonentity even to the nervous teacher, for he never was either a failure or a great success in his studies; he was never in mischief, but neither did he have a cheerful eye and smile. Take him by and large, he might be considered a neuter. But here he was clambering up the ladder. What could it mean?

That he had some definite purpose dawned in the minds of the watchers when he was seen to work on above the halfway mark and still higher and higher toward the platform above which the wheel was spinning and clanking.

"Go up and bring him down! Quick! Quick!" cried Sophie Preston. "He'll fall—he'll be killed!"

The biggest boy in the school ran forward as a volunteer and hurried up a dozen rungs of the ladder until the full force of the wind caught him and flung him hard to one side. Then, with a cry of fear, he looked up just in time to see one of the worn rungs break beneath the feet of

Danny. Poor Danny hung at arm's length and swayed far out in the wind like the flag on the Fourth of July. That was enough for the rescuing hero, for he did not wait to see Danny clutch the ladder again with his legs. He hastened down to firm ground, sick in the pit of his stomach, and from the solid earth he looked up and saw Danny disappear through the trap and clambering onto the storm-swept platform high above.

Here the wind veered and tossed the flying wheel around. Its darting vanes skimmed the very head of Danny, and the teacher, with a scream, covered her face.

"He's all right! Oh, look!" cried one of the older girls to Miss Preston, and when she stared upward again, she saw Danny standing erect on the platform!

More than that, he was reaching toward the fan and tugging fiercely at it.

"Come down!" screamed twenty voices in a wild chorus, but the words were lost and blended in the whistle of the wind, and all that reached Danny was a mere roar. To answer it, he stood on the very edge of the platform and waved down to them.

Thereat Miss Preston fainted away. But she was hardly heeded. The pupils were too busy gazing at Danny as that pudgy form, standing still near the verge of the platform to gain a great purchase on the fan, tugged strongly at it. Finally, as the wind abated for an instant, he was able to jerk it in. The wheel swung around out of the wind, and in a trice Danny, with the broken fragment of rope, had lashed fan and wheel together.

By the time Miss Preston recovered, Danny was on the ground again.

After that, Danny was regarded with new eyes.

"Were you scared?" asked some one, a little later.

"Scared?" said Danny, and his dreamy eyes lighted a little. "Well, I dunno as—"

"He dunno what bein' scared is," said a cow-puncher who heard the report. "That kid'll come to something—or nothing!"

Miss Preston tried to make much of the young hero, but she tried in vain. When she praised him, he looked at her bewildered, and he shook his head.

"It was sort of fun," was all Danny would ever say about that adventure.

For two years, after that, he continued to live his usual [illegible]

who put them tacks on your seat? I done it!"

"Oh!" murmured Danny, and smote his tormentor fairly upon the root of the nose.

There is something immensely disconcerting about a punch on the nose, smartly given. It floods the eyes with tears; it stings like a hornet; and if a trickle of red follows, the weak-hearted lose their nerve. The bully, jumping back, ran a forefinger under his nose and it came away very red. After that he was willing to call the battle off. But Danny Cadigan was only beginning.

He had never fought before. But he had stood by and watched many and many a grisly encounter with his dull black eyes. Those eyes were glittering and gleaming now. He came swiftly in with his left arm extended as he had seen the best boxers in the school always do when they wanted to make an opening. He bashed that left fist into the stomach of the bully and then cracked home his right hand squarely against the chin of the other.

The big boy went down with a thud, and before he could recover, while he was still groaning: "Enough!" Danny Cadigan flung the conquered upon his face and twisted one arm of the fallen into the small of his back. After that, the bully was helpless. The more he struggled, the more agonizing was the pressure that was brought upon his twisted shoulder socket. Suddenly he began to scream, wild, blood-chilling yells.

And the hand of Cadigan was seen to be dipping into a coat pocket and out again, apparently pressing something into the back of the fallen. Half a dozen boys dragged him away. And then it was found that he had been jabbing the tacks of the day before, deep into the body of the unfortunate victim.

The teacher could not believe it until she saw the blood oozing out on the coat of the unhappy youngster. Then she took Danny to one side and talked long and gravely to him.

"I dunno," said Danny. "He stuck me with tacks when I wasn't lookin'. I stuck him with tacks when he *was* lookin'. Is that wrong?"

That was the last fight of Danny Cadigan for ten years. For, during that space of time, he remained near his home town. And, no matter how mild his behavior, rumor went before him and warned ignorant strangers of the danger that lay concealed beneath that mild exterior.

Until his twenty-second year, the windmill and that one fight were the outstanding features in the life of Danny, except for the death of his father and his mother. As for the passing of his father, Danny did not seem to mind it greatly. He was seen beside the grave in his range-rider's costume, just as he had ridden in from the near-by ranch where he was working. He was grown, now, into a youth a little above a middle height, with broad shoulders, and a sleek face, and eyes which looked simply stupid to some, and sad to others.

"They ain't no heart in him," said the rancher for whom he worked. "When I give him word that his pa had died, he just grunted and went on eatin' his dinner. That's the way with that Danny Cadigan!"

Two years later, his mother closed her eyes. But that was very different. Danny came and sat beside the dead body for twenty-four hours, until the doctor came in and tipped up his head and looked down into the dull, expressionless eyes.

"You better get some sleep," said the doctor. "You can't do any good here now, my boy!"

So Danny Cadigan left the room without a word, but not to sleep. And when the body was buried in the grave in the cemetery under the elms, he stood beside the hole with his usual lack-luster eyes. There he remained, too, long after the coffin was covered and the mound completed and the little crowd of mourners scattered away. Some said that he stayed there for a whole day before he went back to the range.

[illegible]

2

AT KIRBY RANCH

North and north and north rode Cadigan, until he came, on a day, into the view of a cow-puncher struggling on the back of a piebald mustang which was leaping off the earth, tying itself into knots in mid-air, and landing again with stiff legs and sickening jolts. At the third jolt, the cow-puncher dived into the corral dust, whereupon the mustang turned and tried to eat his foeman. Cadigan drew rein by the fence, and watched a second hero try and fail. Then, as the others stood back, cursing, none anxious to begin, Cadigan said to the man who appeared to be in control:

"You ain't got a job floatin' around loose, have you?"

At this the rancher turned sharply upon him and noted the sleek skin, the mild black eyes.

"I ain't got a job for you, son," he said harshly. "We ain't started workin' boys up here. This here is a man's range."

He turned away, but added as a cruel afterthought: "Unless you can ride that paint hoss!"

When he looked again, Cadigan had dismounted, thrown his reins, and climbed the fence.

In the first ten minutes Cadigan was thrown three times. Once he was hurled clear over the fence. Twice he escaped the wicked feet or teeth of the horse by rolling under the [illegible]

"He ain't a fightin' man," said Kirby to his boys. "He talked like he was pretty peaceful. Still, we seen him show game in the saddle, and I guess that we can use him for a while. Just handle him easy, boys. He can do the chores while you cut out the big work."

So Cadigan was used for chores on the Kirby ranch. He was given wood chopping, milking, hay pitching, fodder cutting—a brutal labor with a hay saw—and every other odd job around the ranch which required good humor and patience rather than brains or courage.

And all went well on the Kirby ranch so far as Cadigan was concerned. For it was a big country of huge mountains, and mighty pine forests. The cattle grew lofty in stature and thick of bone. And the horses which were ridden at the end of the ropes were twelve hundred pounders, capable of working in a plough team; and the rope itself was a sixty-foot burden. How different from the light, supple thirty-five-foot rope with which your Southwesterner works his cows! And the men on the Kirby ranch were as big as their country. That is to say, they were all proven many times over. Each knew the formidable quality of the other. The peace was that of a drawn battle.

As for Cadigan, they paid no attention to him. Or, if they did, it was only a word or a grunt. He did not mind it when they talked down to him. Therefore there was no friction. No one could have dreamed that trouble would come until Bill Lancaster came into camp and forced the issue.

He went to Kirby and asked for work. Kirby was very polite, because politeness was well known to be a necessity when one addressed Bill Lancaster.

"Certainly," said Kirby. "I'll be mighty glad to have you around. They's a lot of wolves up around my way that been needin' killin' for a long time."

This hint was received by Lancaster with a broad grin, and he rode out to the ranch at the side of Mr. Thomas Kirby, feeling that the world had at least some traces of good sense—in that it knew that Bill Lancaster must always be well received, and at supper that night, Danny Cadigan saw the famous man for the first time. Afterward he talked to Jud McKay.

Jud was the oldest and the most good-natured of the cow-punchers who worked upon the old Kirby place. The others referred to Dan as the "boy." But old Jud McKay called him "son." Perhaps he despised Danny more than the others did. But there was this point of advantage. Danny had not heard his stories before, and all his tales were ancient history to the rest of the working force. Indeed, in the whole section there was hardly a man who did not know the stories of Jud McKay as well as they knew the face of that worthy waddie. It had been five years, well-nigh, since he had spun a yarn to any audience without seeing at least one of them begin to yawn. But in Dan Cadigan he found a perfect listener. For hours on end Cadigan was willing to sit passively and drink in the words of the old cow hand, his dreaming, dull-black eyes fixed on the distance, while Jud McKay fought Indians and dug gold enough to have furnished forth another California.

When they left the supper table, Cadigan was full of wonder and full of doubts. For, during the meal, he had noticed that when Bill Lancaster spoke all the others became silent and even Tom Kirby himself lent an attentive ear. So he cornered Jud McKay at the corral where Jud had gone to look over a Roman-nosed filly which had recently been added to his string. It was dusk of a June day; the stars were coming out singly through the haze of the after-glow, and in the south and east the Chico Range was turning black and drawing huge and near. They leaned on the fence smoking their after-supper cigarettes, enjoying the coolness, for their faces still burned from the fiery heat of the day and ovenlike closeness of the dining room, filled with the odor of fried onions and scorched meat.

[illegible]

"Right," said McKay. "You got sense—about hosses, Danny."

"This here Lancaster—" began Dan Cadigan.

"Oh, him?" said Jud McKay. "What about him?"

"He seems to be quite a man."

Jud McKay shifted his cigarette dexterously from one corner of his mouth to the other, on the tip of his tongue.

"They's enough in him to cut out two men, son," said he, "with all the trimmin's!"

Cadigan waited.

"What's he done?" he said at last.

"Growed-up men," said McKay, "don't ask so doggone many questions. Gimme a chance to think."

He went on, pacified by the apologetic silence of Cadigan: "Lancaster was a tenderfoot. He come out to Montana and put some money into cattle. He was trimmed pretty bad, and when he found out what had happened to his coin, it turned him sort of sour. He didn't run amuck. He just started in to get the gents that had done him. They was five of 'em. He didn't push things along. He just waited until he got the right chance so's he could put the blame on them. Well, two years ago he killed the last of the five. One of 'em skinned out of the country. One of 'em is a cripple for life. Three of 'em is dead. That's the way that Bill Lancaster worked 'em. And he got the taste for that sort of fun. He begun to figure that his time was pretty near wasted if he didn't have a fight on his hands about every month or so. Some day he'll be bumped off, but most likely it'll be with a shot from behind. Because Bill, he don't booze none, and he keeps in training. He fights himself into shape, you might say, all the time!"

To this thrilling account, Cadigan listened with the proper quiet.

"The trouble with Lancaster," said McKay, "is that he likes any sort of fight, big or small. He'd corner a rat and make it bite his foot for the sake of setting that boot on it and hearin' it squeal. He likes to see other gents suffer. That's the way with Lancaster!"

He added; "But you just pipe down mighty small and you'll get in no trouble. Just keep away from Lancaster and when he starts badgerin' you, don't talk back. But if he thinks you're scared of him—he'll never let up on you till—" He cleared his throat and changed the subject abruptly.

"A mean hoss with no sense, and too light in front—it's like investin' a lot of work in bum land that won't give you no crop for all your trouble."

But Cadigan did not answer. He presently drifted away from the corral and headed toward the bunk house. It consisted of one room with a big window at either end and a large stove in the center—a stove which was a vital necessity in the heart of the stern winter and which served as a targe for cigarette butts. The bunks were built against the wall in a double tier, and they were littered with blankets of all colors, faded with dirt and age, gleaming and new, whole and tattered. In the interstices between the bunks, hanging from clusters of nails, were thick bundles of clothing, battered suit cases, wrinkled tarpaulins, and much footgear in various stages of disrepair.

Usually the cow-puncher does not accumulate much old stuff. What is worn out is thrown away. But the men at the Kirby ranch remained long enough to have about them the apparel of three or four years, at the least. Hence the wreckage which made the bunk house look very much like a junk shop.

Cadigan removed his boots and lay down after lighting the lantern at the head of his bunk. He pulled a dog-eared magazine from his blankets and folded it open. But this was only a mask behind which his attention wandered dreamily to other things.

Half of his thoughts were in the past, and half were in the present. Out of the past he was remembering two things [illegible]

seemed to Cadigan that he was not constituted for happiness. Other men could be full of gayety. But the only landmarks in his life were the deaths of his father and of his mother. There was no great soul-possessing happiness excepting, only, those trials by fire—the climbing of the windmill, and the fight in the school yard. What had there been in them? It was danger, and danger only, which intoxicated him with pleasure. It was danger which acted upon the dull, sleepy soul of Cadigan like the sun on a closed flower.

Now Lancaster came, and once more the old tingle of delight began to warm his blood like wine.

His awakening eye glanced to the left and caught on two small holes drilled neatly through the boards of the wall beside his bunk. They had been covered with a nailed plank on the outside to shut out rain and wind. He had never noticed them before. But at some time in the past a revolver must have barked twice in the bunk house. There was absolutely no doubt of it in the mind of Cadigan.

In the meantime, the bunk house was filling gradually with tired cow-punchers who had lounged outside under the growing light of the stars but had finally been driven in to their bunks by the weary ache of their limbs.

"Hello!" cried the voice of Bill Lancaster. "Darned if I ain't forgot my tarpaulin. Ain't there a chore boy here that'll trot out and get it for me?"

3

DANNY AND LANCASTER CLASH

Cadigan, in his bunk, stretched his body slowly until he felt the pull of the muscles from the tip of his fingers down his arms and through his body and along his legs. Then he relaxed again. As a cat relaxes, when it has made itself aware of claws sharp beneath their sheaths of velvet, and of needle-pointed teeth, and of strong jaw muscles.

So it was with Cadigan. And he remembered, now, that his strength had never been fully tested except twice—once when he tugged at the fan of the windmill twelve years ago, and once when he struck the bully fairly in the center of the face a whole decade since. But in the interim, nothing had happened which had developed all of his power. He thought of this and yawned discreetly behind his hand.

"No chore boys here," said old Jud McKay. "You got to run your own errands, Lancaster."

"The devil!" growled out the newcomer. "What sort of an outfit is this here?"

Some one murmured words which Cadigan could not quite hear.

"Oh," said Lancaster. "Is that it? Well, that'll do for me."

Like a shadow sweeping across a pond when the wind [illegible]

gan.

"What's your name?" asked Lancaster.

Cadigan lowered his magazine and turned his head. He surveyed the other from head to foot, slowly, luxuriously, taking note of all his power. Here was danger indeed, vast danger with a cruel horde of possibilities. And once again the thrill of expectant happiness shot through him.

"My name's Dan Cadigan," said he.

"Well, Danny," said Lancaster, "ain't you the roustabout on this here ranch?"

Cadigan turned his head away and looked at the bottom of the bunk above him, as though in thought. But, in reality, he was merely tasting the intense relish of this scene. It was better than feeling that tug and jerking of the invisible hands of the wind; it was better than leaning from the platform of the windmill and waving at the frightened crowd who stood craning at him, a dizzy distance below. For the first time in his life, Cadigan felt an infinite satisfaction coming to him. And this was not all. More was to come!

"I dunno that I ever been called the roustabout," he said gently.

"Look here, kid," said Lancaster. "I don't aim to get riled none. I'm a peaceful man, I am. I'm darned if I like to get my dander up. But I say you're the roustabout, and what I say goes!"

"Yes," said Cadigan softly.

"Ain't you the one that milks the cows and chops the firewood?"

"Yes," said Cadigan.

"And, if you do them things are you too good to run an errand for me out to the stable?"

"I didn't say that I wouldn't run an errand," said Cadigan.

There was an appeased grunt from Lancaster. "Well," said he, "hop up, then, and lemme see some action. That tarp is over in the corner right under my saddle. You can tell my saddle by the silver on it. I want that roll brung in here and put over on my bunk."

He spoke the last words over his shoulder as he turned away, but when he had taken a few steps, he saw that all was not well. He could tell it by the sudden change which had come in the atmosphere of the room. Every man had paused in the very midst of the act which employed him. One had a boot half off; another held the match flaming in his hand without raising it to the tip of the cigarette; another paused with his vest thrown back over his elbows, ready to slip it off. But each stopped short and began to stare with widened eyes. Lancaster turned sharply about and saw that Cadigan had not moved.

He could hardly believe it. Then the wild red blood swelled his face. He was back beside the bunk with a leap.

"Cadigan!" he thundered.

"Yes?" said the gentle voice of Cadigan.

"Did you hear what I told you?"

"Yes," said Cadigan.

"Why ain't you movin'?"

The glance of Cadigan dwelt upon the huge, balled fists of the gun fighter. He could hardly speak, so great was that inward satisfaction.

"I was thinkin' it over," said Cadigan.

And then some one giggled like a girl, hysterically. That sound precipitated the cloudy wrath of Lancaster. No matter what happened, he would have to vent that wrath in physical action before he was through with this scene.

"Get up!" he snarled out.

Cadigan looked up and saw that the eyes of Lancaster were like the eyes of a beast.

"Get up!" gasped out the big man, and leaning a little, he gripped Cadigan by the shoulder.

Into the thick flesh of Cadigan's shoulder the fingers [illegible]

[illegible] an old man. I'm gunna—"

"Hey, Lancaster!" called the shaken voice of old Jud McKay. "Don't make no mistake. That kid ain't no fighter."

Lancaster turned on McKay in a ravening fury. "To the devil with your heart!" he raged. "I ain't gunna stop with the kid, maybe. Maybe I'm gunna go right on and be school-teacher to the whole lot of you. Understand?"

Jud McKay shrank back into the shadow of his own bunk. To his own heart he vowed that if he had been a younger man—but he was not young. He was old, he was stiff, he was weak. Why did not some other among these men stand up to stop the horror which was about to take place? But not a man moved. There were black faces among them. But the danger was too great. This was Bill Lancaster, and at the side of the big man were Bill Lancaster's two guns, each with a half dozen stories sealed in its magazine.

Lancaster wheeled back upon his victim. Cadigan standing was a far different spectacle from Cadigan lying down, or Cadigan sitting. He was exactly ten inches above five feet in his height, and he weighed without his clothes exactly a hundred and ninety pounds, which never varied hot weather or cold, in idleness or in fierce and long-continued labor. He weighed a hundred and ninety, but he looked a full twenty pounds lighter, for that bulk was not noticed in the roundness of his chest and his depth from front to back. But what Lancaster saw at once was that here was a solid fellow—as solid as lead! No one else on the Kirby place had ever suspected it. But Lancaster was not like the others. When one has hunted fights in wholesale quantities, one begins to be able to recognize the fighters. Here, perhaps, was no fighting heart. But certainly here was one who would have stripped well in the prize ring. And Lancaster, remembering how the shoulder flesh had stiffened into thick, gristly muscle, decided suddenly that he would risk no personal encounter. The guns would decide this little matter.

He fell back half a pace.

"I'll tell you what I'll do," said Lancaster. "You apologize and then trot out and get that tarp and I'll let you off. Understand?"

Cadigan blinked.

"D'you hear me?" yelled Lancaster.

Then he heard a startled gasp from all the roomful of spectators. For Cadigan was smiling! And indeed, there was in the body and in the soul of Cadigan such a rioting joy that he could no longer suppress it. It burst forth at his eyes in light. It made the corners of his mouth twitch back, and while he smiled straight into the soul of the larger man, he felt as though he were already grappling the other in spirit.

"By the heavens!" breathed Lancaster, and gliding back another half step, he reached for his gun, which hung behind his right hip.

The fingers gripped the butt, but did not draw the Colt. For the hand of Cadigan darted out and closed over that of Lancaster. It seemed to the killer that a bracelet of fire was clamped upon his wrist, for the wrench of Cadigan's twisting hand fairly ground the flesh against the bones of Lancaster's arm. And the fingers of that good right hand grew numb and helpless.

Lancaster, with a startled cry, jerked himself back, but he could not tear himself away. He was held as though he were chained to a post. And when he reached for his second gun with his left hand, the right fist of Cadigan chopped into his face.

It was like the tap of a sledge hammer, held with a short grip on the handle. It half stunned Lancaster, but it made him desperate, also, and his desperation gave him a power which even the mighty grip of Cadigan could not withstand. The killer tore himself away, reeling back half the

[illegible]

the long weapons came out of their holsters.

At the same time, Cadigan leaped from the floor. His stockinged feet gave him security. He dived as though into water, and his shoulder, striking just above the knees of Lancaster, bowled the big man down like a tenpin. The two guns roared blindly at the same instant. One clipped a new hole through the farther end of the building. And one ripped through the thigh of young Stew Tanner.

Then they crashed to the floor.

Lancaster, as he toppled, reached out and caught the edge of a bunk. That grip could not save him, but the impetus swerved him to one side. He sat half erect, braced against the side of the bunk, and since he did not have time to fire, he chopped the long heavy barrel of his Colt against the head of Cadigan.

And Cadigan went to sleep.

Afterward, Lancaster disentangled himself from the limp arms and hands and rose to his feet. He leaned above the prostrate form with a devil in his face, but there was something electric in the air which made Lancaster look aside, and what he saw in the faces about him told him that it would not be well to touch the helpless body of his late antagonist.

So he stood up again, rubbing his right wrist. It had turned blue and purple and was swelling fast. Lancaster was filled with a shuddering horror. What manner of man was it who possessed a bone-breaking power like this in his fingers?

He could see more distinctly, now, the nature of the danger from which he had escaped. And, last of all, he remembered the smile of Cadigan. It was not a pleasant thought. Men sometimes grin with pure fury as they are about to fall into a conflict, but no one smiles out of the perfect happiness of the heart. There was something beyond the human about it. There was something devilish and cruel.

Lancaster stared around him. Old Jud McKay had risen and was slowly approaching with something in his face which made Lancaster understand that it would be unwise for him to remain long on the Kirby ranch. It would be very unwise! Other men were standing up. Some one began to move toward the door, and Lancaster decided that a hasty exit would be most advisable.

He did not stay for the small details of his belongings. Even his hat was an unnecessary luxury—to one who was about to take a long ride in the dark. And without staying to take up even his fallen revolver, with the other weapon still clutched in his left hand, he marched for the door of the bunk house and through it.

With the cool, thick dark in his face, some of his courage and nerve returned. He turned suddenly on the cowpunchers and thundered at them: "As for the rest of you rats, remember that Bill Lancaster might run across you, one of these days. And when the kid comes to, tell him that the reason I didn't finish him to-night was because I wanted him awake—to see it coming!"

So Lancaster disappeared into the night.

In the morning his horse was gone and his saddle. The Tom Kirby ranch knew him no more. If he left a memory behind him, it was a thing such as none of the cowpunchers cared to speak of. For they had permitted him to commit a shameful wrong in their presence and to escape unharmed afterward.

4

"ADVISED TO DRIFT"

When Cadigan opened his eyes, he was lying on a blanket in the middle of the floor with the rolled coat of some one for a pillow under his head, and with a circle of anxious faces around him—a dozen men with their hats on their heads, their spurs on their heels, their guns at their sides, as though prepared to start for a day of hard riding through dangerous country. And in the center of the circle, kneeling beside him, was no less a person than Tom Kirby.

"If he don't come to," he heard Kirby saying, "we'll ride to the devil and back until we catch that skunk Lancaster and blow him off the earth."

There was a rumble of applause in the midst of which Cadigan sat up. This movement was greeted with a shout of delight. He could not recognize the illumined faces before him as those of the surly, brutal men he had known earlier in that same evening. They clasped his hands, they raised him tenderly to his feet, they bade him lean upon them, they conducted him to a bunk, and they would have stretched him tenderly in it, but here Cadigan protested that there was nothing wrong with him.

"Nothin' but a cracked skull!" said Kirby. "Is that nothin' to you, Cadigan?"

It was almost the first time he had been called anything other than "the kid," or simply, "hey, you!" Cadigan appreciated the difference.

"That's only a small bump," said Cadigan. "It really isn't worth thinkin' about. I can manage myself, gents."

"Good old boy!" said one. "He'll always stand on his two feet!"

But Cadigan wanted to think. He wanted to be by himself. It was a passionate need, and he straightway slipped away into the dark of the outer night and sat down against a sweet-smelling stack of newly put-up hay. There he contemplated all that had happened. It was not altogether in the past. Indeed, there was a great deal still running over into his present. For instance, the fierce and riotous happiness which had been awakened in him was still there in his blood like a liquid fire, was still in his brain and in his heart, and he could have sung—though there had never been music in his throat before through all his life!

When he tried to think back to what had happened, he was baffled, for it was like trying to contemplate two creatures. His old self was one. It had been sleepy, lazy, indifferent to the world. His new self was another. Here was no horse to be ridden, no windmill to be climbed and then relax into sleep after the climbing. Here was far more. The man who had insulted him and struck him down had escaped unpunished, and there remained before him the far greater problem than the hand-to-hand conflict. There remained the unfinished task: He must hunt down Lancaster and master him with the work of his gun which his hands could not complete.

Until that was done, he could never rest content. And that wild work lay before him like an endless fairy tale to which a child can listen forever. For how could he ever hope to master the wonderful dexterity, the long and cruel experience, of Bill Lancaster? He remembered the pale blue eyes of the big man which had blazed at him with cold fury. On what day would he face those eyes again? It was a quiet delight which Cadigan took home to his heart.

Walking back toward the bunk house he was singing softly to himself, and so he almost ran against the figure [illegible]

"I always set you down for a doggone sad one. Maybe all you needed was a little more trouble—a little fightin', Dan, to set you up?"

Dan was silent.

Suddenly the voice of Tom Kirby dropped to a lower note. "Look here, Cadigan," he said, "me and the boys have been talkin' this all over. Well, son, the way it looks to us, we've played a pretty small game with you-all. We've been treatin' you like a kid when you was doggone near the only man among us. Old Jud McKay he spoke up and told us what we was; he says he's the only man that ever seen what was in you. Well, we got to admit that Jud has spent a pile of time with you. Now, Cadigan, the boys all put in and say they want me to tell you that they're mighty sorry for what they done. They all know that they stood around mighty shameful and let Lancaster fight foul. They seen it, and they'd ought to of pulled their guns and shot him dead. Well, they didn't do it. Partly it was because they didn't noways figure that their eyes could be seein' right when they made out Lancaster playin' a dirty trick on a—a young gent like you that ain't always practicin' with his Colt in his spare minutes. And it was partly, to tell you the plain truth, because they was scared to tackle Lancaster, even after they seen the way that you was handlin' him. Maybe you dunno the sort of a name that Lancaster has in these parts, son. But I'll tell you that they ain' no three men that'd hanker to meet up with Lancaster and shoot it out man to man, them all on one side and him all on one side!"

He paused and cleared his throat, having concluded this embarrassing speech.

"It's all right," said Cadigan quietly. "You don't have to do no apologizing. I've forgot all that. It happened pretty quick, too."

"That was it!" exclaimed the rancher hastily, seizing upon this straw with desperate haste. "The way they told me about it, you was as fast as a tiger after him, and he wasn't no slouch himself. It was all one whirl and bang and then there was you down and Lancaster up and sneaking away. Well, Cadigan, the boys figure that they might of done more, anyways. They're eatin' their hearts out because they didn't take a crack at him, and if you'd been bad hurt they wouldn't never of rested till they had rode down Lancaster and finished him—or he finished them!"

The very fact that the rancher included the latter alternative as a possibility convinced Cadigan, if he had needed convincing, that he had seen only a small part of the formidable qualities of Lancaster.

"I know," said Cadigan gratefully, "that they'd of stood behind me. They're mighty kind, Mr. Kirby."

The rancher snorted, but he went on quickly: "About one more thing, son."

"Well?"

"You figure that you're done with Lancaster?"

"Why—not quite."

"You're right! You ain't seen the last of him. You ain't even begun to catch a glimpse of him. I'll tell you why, if you can't guess!"

"I'd sure like to know what you think," murmured the roustabout gently.

"Because you've stood up to him, which is more'n any other man has done for a mighty long time, old son! You've stood up to him, and he ain't apt to forget it. It's what you might call a blot, to Lancaster. He claims to be the doggonedest hard one that ever shot up a town for fun. It'd plumb break his heart to have somebody throw this here mess into his face and tell him about the time that a—a youngster, son, got him on the run. You understand?"

"I see," said Cadigan.

"It's blood, Cadigan!"

"What!"

[illegible]

had appeared on the face of his companion in the dark? For only a glint of light fell upon Cadigan's features from the stars.

"You might be able to sling a gun yourself. But it ain't no ordinary kind of gun fighter that you'd have to be to face Lancaster. Why, son, he killed Harry Worth and Shank Bristol in one fight when they both jumped him—one behind and one in front. He killed 'em both. He shot Worth first. He had two slugs of lead inside of him. He lay on the floor and scooped up his gun with his left hand and killed Bristol with it. Understand?"

There was a low murmur from Cadigan. After that, a pause followed as the rancher allowed his young hired hand to digest all of this important information. Far off, a young colt began to whinny sharply, and the neigh of the grazing mother which had strayed away rang back like a clarion. After that, there was the thick, wide silence of the night around them. From the bunk house there was not a sound. It was as though the calamity of the evening had forced all the punchers to turn in at once and to fall instantly to sleep.

"I got some advice to give you, Cadigan."

"Well, sir?"

"If I was you, I'd ride south doggone fast. I'll loan you a hoss."

"Why?"

"My heavens!" cried the other. "Do I have to tell you that—now? What sort of a crazy man are you, son? I tell you, unless you get out of the way, Lancaster will get you. They ain't no possible manner of way to doubt that!"

"Thanks a lot," said Cadigan in his usual gentle manner. "I'll certainly have to think about all of this."

With this, he stood up and sighed. Or was it, as it seemed to Tom Kirby, a mere yawn? At any rate, Cadigan went into the blackness of the bunk house and Tom Kirby went on, after a time, into his own domicile.

He was very gloomy. Often he paused on his way and cursed freely with a liberal and well-educated tongue, which had been improved by constant practice cutting out recalcitrant calves. And what can compare with a calf for the exercise of a man's vocabulary.

When he reached the big ranch house, his wife knew that there was trouble in the mind of her lord by the manner in which he slammed the door behind him. Also, she heard the faint echoes as he cursed the cook; and from the lower hallway she could hear him cursing his house, his family, his cow hands, his ranch, the state in general, the West from north to south, the country at large, the entire globe, the solar system, the starry universe. He consumed space by a thousand light years at a stride as he rose to the second floor of the dwelling.

He came into the bedroom trailing a cloud of silent fury behind him. Therefore Mrs. Tom Kirby, who was very young, very pretty, and wiser than she was fair, greeted him with a pleasant smile and not a word.

When he slumped into a chair with a grunt, she rose from her place beside the window where she had been letting the cool of the evening breeze ruffle her hair, and going to the man of the house, she removed from his head the towering, massive sombrero which he had forgotten to take off, and then she wiped his heated forehead. Still she said nothing. And, by degrees, the knots disappeared from his forehead. She went back to her chair and turned it softly around so that it faced him.

Nothing is so irritating to a man as not to be noticed by his womenfolk when he is in a passion. Nothing does he love so much as to be awful in their sight! Mrs. Tom Kirby was entirely willing to be awed now and then. After all, it was a small price.

So she waited, attentive, gentle, faintly smiling her sympathy, brooding fondly upon her husband's face, but yet not quite so fond as she appeared. She saw, by degrees, the storm cloud lifted

[illegible]

"I said," she answered hastily. "Aren't you unhappy tonight?"

He grunted, then decided that he *could* not have heard aright the first time, and proceeded to unburden his mind.

"What's wrong? Please!" said Mrs. Tom.

"A dead man!" said he gloomily.

"Tom!"

"I said it."

"Who?"

"Cadigan."

"Good heavens, Tom, the boy isn't dead? Oh, you don't mean it!"

"He will be!"

"Let me go to him!"

"I mean, he's gunna be got by Lancaster."

"Oh, is that all?"

"Ain't it enough? Don't seem to be no logic in you women."

"Of course," admitted Mrs. Tom Kirby tactfully, "we aren't men."

Her spouse grunted. "I told the young blockhead about Lancaster. I told him to start south—pronto. Well, what d'you think that he did?"

"I can't guess!" said Mrs. Tom wisely.

"He just yawned. Darned if he didn't act like I'd told him that Lancaster wore yaller shirts, or something like that. Didn't seem no ways interested. And when he went into the bunk house afterward, I hear him hummin' to himself. The young fool maybe thinks because he knocked Lancaster down that he could beat him even with guns. Darned if it ain't laughin' at a rattlesnake because it can't bite through stone!"

"Of course. How terrible!"

"It is. He's dead. If he had folks, I'd tell 'em to order mournin' now. But he ain't got none."

"An orphan?"

"Him? Sure."

"No relatives in the world?"

"Nobody, from what he says. He's in a one-man canoe, up to now. Doggone lucky at that!"

Did Mrs. Tom understand the secret thrust in the last sentence? She did. For she answered sweetly:

"Poor child!"

"Hey, wait a minute!" exclaimed her spouse. "He ain't as young an' helpless as all that! Keep some of that sympathy to spend on the first of the month. Maybe *I'll* need it."

MEETING UNCLE JOE LOFTUS

If Sunday is a dull day in town, it is the incarnation of boredom on a cattle ranch. Hence the weekly migration of cow-punchers on Saturday night toward any center of lights and voices to fortify themselves against the silence of the "day of peace." But on Sunday morning, there were two in the bunk house. One was old McKay who had lost all his money playing blackjack with Kirby on Wednesday night, and one was Cadigan, for whom towns had no more attraction than the open country.

Cadigan listened to a story of prospecting days in which he heard, again, how McKay had had millions in his hands, only to lose them through the crookedness of a partner. He listened from eight o'clock until ten-thirty. Then he spoke on his own behalf.

"Who's the best shot in these parts, Mr. McKay?"

The "mister" always pleased McKay. It was partly a tribute to his years; he felt that it was even more a tribute to his exceptional character.

"Why, I s'pose that Steve Atwater is about the best.

Steve is fast and pretty accurate. Tom Kirby ain't no slouch himself. And I've always had my day."

"Atwater is the best?"

"Take him for speed and score together. Atwater is about the best. They ain't no more like there used to be—except this Lancaster, you might say. Lancaster is poison. He's like some of the old-timers. Pretty near!"

"No old-timers left?"

"You mean them that *couldn't* miss?"

"Yes."

"They're all gone, son. They're mostly dead. Nobody ever shot too straight and too quick to get dropped some day. Nobody but Uncle Joe Loftus."

Cadigan stroked the bandage which encircled his head, where the gash which the heavy barrel of Lancaster's gun had made was fast healing.

"Loftus? I've heard a little about him. He was a pretty well-known man in the old days, I guess."

"Oh, the whole doggone country knowed Loftus. Loftus is the one that the president made marshal in the days of the Murchison gang. He got the whole gang. He done it pretty near all by himself, too. I'd say that Loftus was pretty well known. He was a killer, and he lived past his killin' days. Even right now, I guess they ain't nobody that would go trailin' Uncle Joe. Maybe his hand ain't too steady. But his brains, they don't shake none!"

He chuckled over the thought, rocking himself back and forth on the box which served him as a chair. For real chairs did not last long in the bunk house.

"Well," said Cadigan, "how old is Uncle Joe Loftus, if you might happen to know?"

"I dunno," said McKay, "that anybody knows how old Uncle Joe is. I dunno that he knows himself how old he is. About all he could do is to guess. He reckons time by 'before the war' and 'after the war'."

"Which side did he fight on?"

"Both!" said McKay, and laughed again. "They ain't nobody like Uncle Joe!"

"I hear that he lives over in the Chico Mountains?"

"Right under the left shoulder of Chico Mountain itself."

"He was fast and straight shootin', both?"

"Lightnin'—and straight as a string. I could tell about when he met up with the two oldest Murchison boys—"

It was noon before that story was ended by the merci- [illegible]

caster has got his own dose of lead and has gone to sleep. Then you come back up here. You ain't goin' to be forgot in these parts, Cadigan!"

All of which came from the heart, so that Cadigan could not without embarrassment confess that this was not exactly what he had planned to do. He received his pay and mounted an old bay gelding which was presented to him by Kirby—"for luck" and perhaps also because it was badly broken down in front.

So, having made his pack and strapped it behind his saddle, he shook hands with McKay and jogged off south with the last words of McKay still ringing in his ears.

"If you should ever meet up with Lancaster, remember that he ain't the kind that's got to shoot twice. He ain't goin' to drill you through no leg or through no place in the body so's you'll have a chance to get in your own bullet. His first shot is his last one. He kills with it!"

With this solemn warning to guide his action, Cadigan jogged the old gelding south for half a dozen miles. Then he turned almost east, keeping for a landmark and a goal straight before him the broad face and the lofty head of Mount Chico.

In the middle of the afternoon, he passed through a small town and there, even though it was Sunday, he was able to buy all the ammunition which he could load upon his gelding. After that, he went on again, and he came, an hour before sunset, in view of the place.

It was a little shack set out on the bald shoulder of the

mountain, surrounded, at a distance, by a scanty growth of lodge-pole pines, those hardy pioneers of forests and heralds of the coming of the great trees. A spring broke from the side of the mountain a little distance away. And so there was ample provision for such a man as Uncle Joe Loftus. His rifle could kill his game. His traps could catch enough pelts to supply him with flour and ammunition. And, for the rest, he worked as he had done for the past thirty years, in a vain endeavor to locate a fabulous lead of copper ore in the Chico Range—a famous secret mine from which, it was said, the Indians in the ancient days had brought down great chunks which were eighty-five per cent pure copper. For that vast wealth the old fellow was still hunting, patiently, counting his progress by decades, still recombing the old ground and patiently plotting out the new. One could hardly believe that such a fighting man could have settled down to such a lonely, dull life!

Or was it dull? Perhaps, thought Cadigan, the hunt for the hidden mine was like a man trail—with this difference—that it promised to have no ending. One might as well have been following a ghost.

As he came up, walking and leading his horse, for the poor thin brute had been exhausted by its heavy pack and the long climb up the side of the mountain—he saw a thin old man come to the door of the shack and shade his eyes against the flare of the western light to peer at the stranger. It was a tall figure, with clothes hanging loosely on the fleshless bones, and a large head set uneasily on a scrawny neck which had been withered away to bones and sinews and windpipe. Age had taken his teeth, and now his strong and cruelly outthrust chin curved up almost to meet the downward hook of the long red nose.

And his head was as bald as a billiard ball!

One could not have called Uncle Joe a prepossessing figure. He seemed to Cadigan very like a standing skeleton. His toothlessness and his deeply wrinkled skin gave him the appearance of an endless broad grin. As a matter of fact, it was said of him that he never smiled.

This legend and other tales came into the mind of Cadigan as he approached the old hero. When he came close, he stopped. His horse paused with a grunt of relief behind him, and Cadigan bade the old fellow good evening.

Uncle Joe Loftus wasted no time on foolish inquiries concerning the well being of the stranger. He merely said

[illegible]

"Nothin' particular."

"Maybe you ain't aimin' to do no trappin', eh?"

"Not any," said Cadigan truthfully.

"Nor do prospectin', eh?"

"Not a bit. I never learned how to read rocks, Uncle Joe."

"Uncle the devil!" said the irate old man. "How come you're a nephew of mine?"

"I thought," said Cadigan, "that they all called you by that name."

"You thought wrong as the devil," said the old prospector. "You just gimme my own name and not none that was loaned to me by a lot of fools like—" Here he paused, but it was not hard to put "you" into the pause. "You don't know nothin' about rocks and ores, then?" he went on, glaring balefully at Cadigan.

"Not a thing."

"Ain't you been raised in these parts?"

"Why, round about, you might say."

"And you don't know nothin' about minin'? You wouldn't recognize gold, maybe, if you seen it?"

"Why, I s'pose that I would."

"You only s'pose, eh? Well, partner, I dunno that you and me is goin' to get along very well up here together on the same mountain. They ain't much room, you see."

"It looks to me," said Cadigan, "as though there's room for a whole army up here."

"That don't show no good sense," said Uncle Joe more sternly than ever.

"Why not? Ain't there miles and miles of open up here?"

"What're miles and miles, young man, to a couple of gents that can't get on with each other?"

"What should keep us from gettin' on with each other, Mr. Loftus?"

"Talkin' pretty like that and callin' me mister—that don't mean nothin' to me, neither. Nothin' at all! I'll tell you why we don't get on well together. It's because I was born and raised to hate a liar like I hate a rattler. You savvy, son?"

"How come that I've lied none to you?"

"You ain't?"

"Not a bit," said Cadigan thoughtfully, looking back over all that he had said. He could remember nothing in the slightest degree mistaken in any of his speeches, however.

"You ain't lied to me, then?"

"I said not a bit!"

"You said that you ain't come up here to shoot?"

"I said that."

"Neither to hunt nor to trap nor to—prospect none?"

"I said all of that, too."

"And that's the truth, is it?"

"All gospel, Mr. Loftus."

"Well, man, why in the devil *did* you come up here, then? What brung you all the way up the side of Mount Chico with a tired horse?"

"Oh," said Cadigan with a sigh of relief. "Is that all that's botherin' you? You want to know what would bring me up here, Mr. Loftus? Well, sir, I come all this way just for the sake of seein' you!"

This complimentary speech was uttered by Cadigan with a broad smile of pleasure, for surely, he thought, it must serve to conciliate the stubborn old man. But Mr. Loftus, after staring at the young stranger for a moment, replied to his compliment by reaching inside his door and jerking into view a long and ponderous rifle, of a make so thick, so heavy, and so old, that it was a wonder that his skinny old arms could bear up its burden. Yet he shifted it easily enough, letting the barrel fall over the crook of his left arm while the forefinger of his right hand curved around the trigger.

"If that's what brung you up here," he said savagely. [illegible]

6

THE RIO GRANDE FOR CADIGAN

The invitation to depart was not uttered by old Loftus in the easy tone of one who can be profitably smiled at. There was a ring that sent a shiver down the small of Cadigan's back. Nevertheless, he did not depart—neither did he so much as turn around. He remained standing and confronting the hero of a past age.

"You hear me?" yelled Loftus.

"I hear you," said Cadigan gently.

"Then, darn your eyes," screamed Loftus, growing more and more excited as the conversation continued, "you know that you're mighty close to gettin' a slug through your head. Nothin' but the head. I don't shoot squirrels no other way!"

But Cadigan folded his arms and shook his head. "It ain't goin' to go," he said. "It ain't goin' to work, Mr. Loftus," said he.

"Why not? What ain't goin to work?"

"This here bluff."

"My heavens, young man," cried Loftus, trembling with the strength of his fury. "Are you aimin' to drive me plumb wild?"

"No, sir, but I know something about you, and I know that you ain't the kind of a gent that'll shoot down a man, in cold blood. You've had your killin's and plenty of 'em, but you ain't never killed except in a fair fight, and you're [illegible]

to leave. Is that the way of it?"

"That's the way of it."

"Ain't you got no shame, young man?"

"Not a bit," said Cadigan.

"And you don't aim to do nothin' but hang around up here and spy on me and try to find out what I'm locatin' in the line of that copper lead that—"

"Copper?" exclaimed Cadigan, as the truth broke in on him. "Is that the reason that you don't want me around up here? On account of that copper mine? Why, Mr. Loftus, I ain't interested in copper, none!"

"You ain't?" sneeringly inquired the old fellow. "Money don't make no difference to you, I guess. Maybe you're a nephew of God, or something like that, that don't need no coin. Is that the way of it?"

"Right now," said Cadigan bluntly, "money don't mean a thing."

"Maybe you'll gimme a hint," said Loftus dryly, "about what *does* make a difference to you?"

"Sure, I'll let you know, right enough," said Cadigan frankly. "Keepin' alive is the main thing that I'm interested in now."

A light broke upon the face of Uncle Joe. "Ah!" said he. "All you're doin' is to run away from something?"

"I dunno that I'm runnin' away."

"What might you call it, then?"

"Well, the main thing is that I seen I needed help, and so I come up here to you."

Uncle Joe dropped the butt of his rifle to the ground and broke into a strange, cackling laugh. "Doggone if you ain't got me beat," said he. "You come up here to get *me* to help you?"

"That's it."

"Maybe you think that you can get me to go down and fight your fights for you?"

"No," said Cadigan, "But you could teach me how to fight."

This suggestion came to Uncle Joe Loftus in a different way.

"I see," said he. "If they corner you, you want to be able to give some sort of an account of yourself."

"That's right."

"How many is they of 'em?" asked the old man, showing a trifle more interest than before.

"They's only one."

"One! And you runnin' away? The devil, young man, I change mind about you every two seconds. Doggoned if I don't!"

"You see," said Cadigan in his usual gentle voice, "I've used rifles and I've used revolvers about as much as most folks. But I ain't never done no fightin', and I ain't never done no practicin' for fightin'. And this gent that I've met up with, he's about as bad as ten men rolled into one."

"Who might he be? They ain't much chance that I'd know about him, though. They don't breed the sort of men nowadays that a man would hear about livin' up here the way I do, gettin' a mite of news once a year!"

"His name is Lancaster."

"Not Bill Lancaster, young man?"

"Have you heard tell about him?"

"Am I deaf? Am I dumb?" asked the other irately. "Have I heard tell about Bill Lancaster? I'll tell a man that I've heard tell about him. Doggone my hide, are *you* mixed up with *him?*"

All the serious advice of Tom Kirby had not had the force which was put into the singular emphasis with which the old fellow uttered the two pronouns.

"I am," said Cadigan.

"Then—God help your soul, young man. Why are you hangin' around up here where Bill often camps out, you might say. Why ain't you ridin' hell-bent south, where he don't never go, you might say. Why ain't you across the [illegible]

"No, sir."

"Lemme hear why it is, then?"

"I want to hunt down Lancaster."

Joe Loftus threw up both of his hands with a groan of amazement. "Hunt Lancaster!" he yelled.

"There was only one man in the world that could teach me enough to gimme a chance agin' Lancaster. I knew that man was you. Even in his best day, they say that Lancaster wouldn't of been no more'n a mouthful for Uncle Joe Loftus."

"Oh," said Uncle Joe without too much modesty, "I dunno about that. But do they still remember me down below?" He pointed, as though the inhabited world were an infinite distance beneath his place of abode.

"Every man of 'em knows about you, Mr. Loftus. Even me—I come from a mighty ways farther south. They'd all heard about you down there, too. That's why I come up here to you to get help."

"What sort of help, young man?" said Uncle Joe, greatly mollified.

"Teachin' about how to handle a gun."

"Here's a rifle," said Uncle Joe. "Shoot me that branch in two, yonder—that right-hand branch of that there little bush, over yonder."

"I can never hit it," said Cadigan to his soul, and he dropped upon one knee.

For a long five minutes he steadied his rifle upon the

twig. For the light was dull, and the dusk was thickening. Finally he fired, and from the head of the slender shrub one side of the branches were cut away.

"That's it," said Joe Loftus. "You can shoot straight. You'd ought to make a name for yourself at one of these here target contests. You'd get all sorts of silver cups, I'd say!"

He turned and pointed in another direction. "Look at that tin can. Pull out your revolver and punch a hole through it, will you?"

Cadigan drew out his revolver. Something told him that he had not pleased the old fellow any too well with his first experiment as a marksman. He must do better this time. He certainly must not fail of his mark no matter what happened! So the heavy Colt balanced long in his hand. Then he fired and his heart leaped with happiness as he saw the can knocked whirling for a dozen yards across the mountain-side.

He put up his weapon and turned expectantly to Loftus, wondering what sort of praise the prospector would select for him. But instead, Uncle Joe Loftus leaned upon his rifle and stared for a long time at the ground.

"I dunno," said he at the last. "I been hopin'. I been tryin' to figure out some way, but I guess that they ain't none. I guess that they ain't any way that it can be done! I used to disbelieve 'em when they said that a good shot was born and not made. But I guess that they was tellin' the truth."

"Is they no hope for me, Uncle Joe?"

Uncle Joe sighed and shook his head. "I've seen bad shots and bad shots," he said. "But doggone me if you ain't the worst. Gimme a gent that can't hit nothin'. I'd take a chance on doin' somethin' with him. I'd train him for speed like a lightin' flash. But take a gent like you, that can hit *anything,* and they ain't a hope for him. Look here, and I'll tell you why. When I was in my prime, son, I couldn't do no better for accuracy than you done just now. I couldn't do no better then. I dunno that I could even do as good as you for shootin' right now. Lemme see—"

He threw the heavy old rifle lightly into the hollow of

his shoulder. He supported the barrel with a wobbling left hand, and the muzzle of the gun wavered crazily in a futuristic circle. Only for an instant—then the gun exploded and the other twig disappeared from the head of

[illegible]

"Well," he said, "it looks like I still could hit something! Just now and then."

He went on: "But as I was sayin', son, they ain't no hope for a gent that's slow—and hits the mark. Because he's gunna keep aimin'. And a gent that keeps aimin' is sure to make a bum fighter."

"What do you mean?" murmured Cadigan, bewildered.

"What I say, son."

"But don't a man have to aim if he wants to hit anything?"

"Aim?" said the strange old man. "Aim? Why, it's thirty year or more since I aimed a gun! Nope. Not in fightin' you don't take no aim."

"What *do* you do, then?"

"What do you do? You up and shoot a man dead, and that's all that they is to it!"

Cadigan shook his head. If this was the way of it, it was hopeless for him to even attempt to learn.

"How does a gent go about it?" asked Cadigan sadly.

"They ain't no trick to it," said the old prospector. "All you got to do is to start right in and practice a couple of hours a day and keep that up for a couple of years. And then, if you got it born in you anyways, you might make something of yourself, if you got any luck along with you. Because you need luck to get through your first couple of fights, no matter how doggone well trained you might be. That's all that they is to it, young man."

"Is they no hope for me?" asked Cadigan sadly.

"Nope. They ain't no hope at all. This here Bill Lancaster, even the way folks used to figger men, he would of been a fighter in the old days, even. And you, son—darned if you wouldn't of been slow even among the worst of the worst clodhoppers that ever I seen. Darned if you wouldn't of been!"

And, with this, he turned and strode slowly back toward his shack. At the door he turned again toward the downcast figure of Cadigan.

"The Rio Grande, Cadigan. That's the best thing for you!"

7

A HARSH INSTRUCTOR

Uncle Joe Loftus returned from his morning trip with hammer and hope about the middle of the afternoon, very hot, very hungry, and disgustingly shaky about the knees. It was no longer a time when Uncle Joe could trudge about the mountains with a swinging stride, up hill and down, all day, without food, without water, even, and come home as erect as ever, with only his belt drawn a little tighter and his jaw set a little harder. Now he had to watch his strength carefully, like a general conducting an offensive campaign with a dwindling army. It would not do to waste men recklessly, in such a campaign; and it would not do for Uncle Joe to waste his meager store of strength.

For, no matter how optimistically he viewed matters, he was forced to see that his days were numbered. He might have, say, ten years remaining to him. But those ten years would have to be divided. Suppose that it required another three years before he found the great lead —there would then remain to him only seven years during which he could enjoy the glory and the wealth which would flow in upon him for that discovery. But even those seven years would be shortened greatly if he did not take care to husband his resources.

So he kept these matters all in his mind while he was laboring among the mountains. He started early in the day, and he kept to his work until noon or a little later, for in the morning his strength was at its prime, but when the heat of the day came on, his powers faded rapidly. So he always avoided hard wark of any kind in the middle of the afternoon.

Now, as he returned to his shack, shaking his head because of the way in which his knees sagged beneath his weight as he went up the slope, he heard the steady cracking of a revolver in the distance.

At one-minute intervals the gun exploded. It was like a signal, repeated constantly. So he went down the slope to make his inquiries. What he saw, when he came through the screening lodge-pole pines, was Cadigan walking up and down in the midst of a large clearing, with a revolver in his hand. He covered fifty paces, he wheeled suddenly, and fired the instant his gun came in line with a small white rock on the hillside. Then he proceeded slowly to the farther side of the clearing, wheeled, fired again, observed the result, and shook his head. For, every time, he missed!

Then he took his stand in the middle of the clearing, leveled his weapon, and opened a point-blank fire. And every bullet struck fairly on the face of the white rock! There was no doubt about it. When he had once obtained the range, or if he took his time at the mark, he was a deadly shot.

But how much time he needed!

He began to pace back and forth once more, and at the end of his walk still turned to fire at the rock, but the old prospector saw the first knocked up far, far away from the target. He was missing, and he was not missing narrowly, for his bullets were flying ten feet from the mark!

So old Uncle Joe Loftus sat down, hugged his knees in his skinny arms, and laughed long and silently. After that, he rose to his feet and said dryly: "I see that you made up your mind to take advice, young man. You aim to start practicin' for two hours a day?"

"For ten," said Cadigan.

[illegible]

because it was one of his own chiefest virtues and he liked it.

"Why," he went on, "d'you want to stay up here on the mountain to do your practicin'?"

"Because," said Cadigan, "it'll be harder for him to find me up here for one thing. Besides, it's cheap livin' here, and I won't have to spend nothin' much for anything except ammunition. But the best thing of all is that I'm pretty close to you, Mr. Loftus."

"What might you learn from me?" said the old man sullenly. "I ain't teachin' no school up here where the folks can learn how to do murder fine and safe and easy!"

"Of course you ain't," admitted Cadigan. "But when a gent has too much knowledge, he can't help some of it overflowin' now and then. Y'understand?"

Uncle Joe could not keep from smiling. "Well," said he, "lemme tell you something. The best way to start out is to start just swingin' the gun without doin' no firin'! Look here!"

He stood up in the center of the clearing, a tall, gaunt form, the wind blowing his flannel shirt close to his body which seemed to be an arch of hollow ribs alone. And he whipped out his revolver and pointed it at the rock. He whirled around, pivoting on his feet swiftly, and covered the rock again with his revolver.

"D'you see, Cadigan? It ain't how many times you shoot. It's just gettin' in the habit of wishin' the other gent dead. And, every time you pull your gun, say to yourself: 'Lancaster!' Y'understand?"

Cadigan nodded, smiling faintly. This was indeed a clean-handed logic which he could easily comprehend.

"And when you point, point with your forefinger—pull the trigger with your second finger. That's the way. Mostly nobody can shoot straight—and fast! Most everybody can point straight—and fast as a wink. For why? For because a gent that's got a gun and is tryin' to aim is thinkin' mighty hard about what he's doin'. And thinkin' spoils shootin'. Does a cat think when it reaches out and sticks a claw into your hand? No, sir, that cat don't do no thinkin'. But you think about gettin' your hand out of the way, and that's why you can't budge it. No, sir, that hand of yours is tied right down to the spot, compared to the speed of the way that cat hauls off and sticks the claws in. That's the way you got to learn to shoot. You got to stop thinkin' about what you're doin'. You got to start in just killin'. The other things will foller along in line. But that's the way that you got to start!"

Such was the first and the greatest lesson for Cadigan, the most important of all that he ever received, and there were many of them. For the old man was full of his subject, and when he found in Cadigan the patience to execute advice as well as the humility to take it, he was willing to unburden himself of quantities of lore.

To him, gun play was no vulgar thing. It was an art almost divine in its possibilities. It was a thing over which he had brooded during a long lifetime, and which he still found complicated and wonderful. So that in speaking of gun work, the old prospector could only speak his information and his feeling by degrees.

It was the beginning of a regular course in instruction for Cadigan. Never a singing teacher worked over a pupil with more enthusiasm than did old Joe Loftus over this youth. And never did a singing teacher labor over the scales and all the dull tone work of a pupil more than Joe Loftus labored to perfect the technique of Cadigan.

"They's only one way with a gun," said Uncle Joe at least half a dozen times a day, "and all the other ways is the ones that dead men have used. Me, speakin' personal,

I always used the right ways. And so I'm still alive. I've seen a lot o' mighty talented gents with guns. I've seen fast gents on the draw. I've seen gents that could shoot as straight as a string, but soon or later, what happened to [illegible]

A gun that goes into the holster smooth will come out smooth. A gun that goes in fast and smooth'll come out fast and smooth. But a gun that goes in, slow or fast, with a jerk, will come out with a jerk, and a gun that comes out with a jerk, it sure can't shoot straight, and you can lay all your coin on that!"

Such were the lessons which Cadigan received. There was no question of mastering them perfectly. The exactions which the stern old prospector made were so great that it was like attempting to master oil painting. Perfection became a sheer impossibility. It seemed out of the question.

But the progress of Cadigan, even in the estimation of Joe Loftus, was astounding. Because, as he had promised, he actually worked with his guns for ten hours a day. And when the revolver was not in use at a target or going through a drill, it was still the constant companion of Cadigan. He used it as he went over its working parts. Every day it received a thorough cleaning, which was much needed after the work which it was given to do. And these daily tasks of taking the gun apart and assembling it again, gave him a feeling of perfect understanding of the weapon such as he had never had before. He finally came to a point after which he could assemble his revolver in the dark.

This was only one phase. All of the main work had to do with the actual drawing of his gun from a holster, in the first place, and its discharge at a mark. And ah, how bitterly discouraging were many of those days! In the heat of the afternoon, when old Joe Loftus returned from his work, Cadigan had to go through his paces beneath the eye of that stern taskmaster. And in those times, every move he made was wrong, it seemed! From day to day there was no progress. There was nothing in the way of a word of praise. It was always the sharp, snarling voice of Loftus pointing out errors.

"How many times do I have to tell you? Ain't you got no memory? Ain't you got no brains?" Uncle Joe would wail at him. "Doggone me if it ain't disgustin'. Eddication is what all you young gents need. Eddication is what you need, but heaven help them that have to do the teachin' of you! That is all I have to say."

And still the labor went on. It was not a week or a fortnight. For four bitter months he worked, as he had said, ten hours a day. And when his wrist was numb with the labor of handling the revolver, he had to turn to his rifle and work with it.

It was late in October before, on a day, Uncle Joe Loftus said, as he sat in the door of his shack: "You see this here can, Mr. Cadigan?"

"I see it," said Cadigan.

"Well, then, put that gun in your holster."

The gun was obediently disposed of in the required way.

"Now, Cadigan, this here can is Bill Lancaster. I'm gunna throw this here can away. If it hits the ground before you sink a slug in it, you're a dead man, Cadigan."

Cadigan sighed. "All right," said he.

The can snapped out of the hand of Uncle Joe Loftus. It shot behind Cadigan. He wheeled like a flash, the revolver snapping out of the holster, and the gun exploded —the can, in the very act of striking the ground, was caught by the big slug and hurled to a distance.

And the first word of praise escaped from the thin lips of Uncle Joe. "That's pretty near what I'd call shootin'," he said.

"This here can, Cadigan, is Bill Lancaster."

He picked up another. "Kill him, Cadigan!"

And he tossed the can high into the air, as hard as he could fling it.

It shot high up and hung in the sun, a winking, flashing disk of light.

"Shoot!" cried Loftus.

And Cadigan fired. There was a clang far above. The [illegible]

behind the can and spat at it small showers of dirt which sent it rolling swiftly up the slope. Then four bullets emptied from his right-hand gun drove the can still higher. Every bullet had entered the soil a scant inch behind the can. He turned and faced the old man again.

"What's next?" asked Cadigan, as he began to load his revolvers for a fresh attempt.

"The next thing," said Uncle Joe, "is to sit right down here."

Cadigan, prepared for a hard lecture, sighed again and then reposed himself on the doorstep beside his tutor.

"Cadigan," said the old man, "you're a good hand with a gun. You shoot like every can was Lancaster. And if every can was Lancaster, Lancaster would of been a hundred times dead. Cadigan, you're as good a hand with a gun as I ever seen!"

Cadigan could only stare.

"Because," went on Loftus, "they ain't no fear in you. A scary gent, he can't have no luck with a gun. The first time I seen you, I seen that you had the makin's of a first-class shot in you. I could tell it by the way that you stood up here and looked into the eye of my rifle. You didn't change no color. I knowed then what could be made out of you."

"You kept pretty quiet about it," said Cadigan, grinning with joy. "Can I start for Lancaster now?"

"They ain't no man in the world that you couldn't start for now," said Uncle Joe gravely.

8

THE SEND-OFF

When Dan Cadigan prepared to depart in the chill of the next morning, Uncle Joe came forth to see him off, and he brought with him two revolvers whose age was well expressed by the finger-worn appearance of the handles.

"What," said he to Cadigan, "might you say to them two guns?"

"I'd say," said Cadigan, "that they was old Colts."

"Take hold on 'em," said the old man.

Cadigan received them gravely.

"Try 'em," said Uncle Joe.

Cadigan looked about him for a fitting target, and as he looked and paused, three heavy-winged crows dropped out of the top of the pines and flapped across the clearing. Cadigan snapped up the guns and fired. The leader dipped its head and dove straight down into the earth. The second bird whirled in a dizzy circle and began to descend, squawking a harsh protest against fate. Cadigan blew out its life with a third bullet.

"Mighty sweet, straight-shootin' guns," said Cadigan.

“Fair to middlin’, fair to middlin’,” said Uncle Joe. “Do they look like other guns to you?”

“They’re a mite heavier, and they’re longer in the barrel.”

[illegible]

weaklings!” And he regarded the round wrists of Cadigan, corded with tendons of steel.

“They’re just heavy enough,” said Cadigan, “to make a gent know that he has something in his hands.”

“Cadigan,” said his friend gravely, “you got sense. You got more sense than even I give you credit for. Them are the guns that’s been friends to me for these many years—darn if I hardly know how long! No, Sir, they’ve gone to sleep with me and watched over me like a pair of bulldogs. They’ve never had to bark and bite at the same gent more’n once or twice together!” He chuckled evilly. “They was a long time,” said he, “when I figured that the day was sure to come when I’d be cornered and got.”

He nodded, thoughtfully thinking back to those wild times. “And I always figgered that when I went down, I’d be pumpin’ this pair of guns to the last half second. Well, Danny, I’ve turned old and rusty and they ain’t much chance of me bein’ got. Seems like them that used to hate me have took pity on an old, old man!”

He grinned again with infinite malice. “Howsomever, they ain’t botherin’ me none, and I guess that they ain’t much chance that I’ll be bothered none before I pass out in the next year or two.”

“You have thirty years,” said Cadigan tactfully.

“Don’t be a fool, young man!”

“I heard tell about an Indian down in New Mexico that

lived to be more'n a hundred and twenty years old. If a Indian can do it, why can't a white man?"

"Why?" said the old man, grinning more broadly and more happily than ever, "I always said there was nothin' a redskin could do that a white man couldn't do better. You got sense, Cadigan. Well, to get back to them guns. I always have figgered them in the hands of some gent that knew how to fight, and that would die fighting, with his body drilled clean through half a dozen times, and his legs tore to bits, smashed into a corner of a room, maybe, and with a dozen gents shootin' at him—but still with a gun in each fist—fightin' back—still killin' to the last minute."

His voice had raised to a sort of shrill shout of fury as he painted his picture. Then, in lowered tones, he added: "That was how my partner, old man Jeff Gilky, died. I come in too late. But I seen five gents bleedn' bad, all wounded so's they'd never forget it, layin' around on the floor, and I seen three dead men that was lookin' at the ceilin' and wonderin' what it was all about, most like, while they dropped down below like buzzards out of the sky—dropped down to the devil like the murderin' skunks that they was!"

His voice trembled. Then he cleared his throat and added: "It ain't goin' to be my luck to die like that."

"You'll die rich, which is a pile better," suggested Cadigan. "You'll find the copper and you'll be one of the biggest of 'em all. They ain't goin' to leave you out of history, Mr. Loftus."

At this, the eye of Uncle Joe appreciably brightened, but he eventually shook his head sadly. "You hear this from me," he said. "They ain't nothin' worth a good death. I'd give all the copper there is for the sake of dyin' with my boots on the way that a man had ought to. And these here guns, Cadigan, they'd ought to go to a gent that's gunna die that way."

Cadigan started. "Am I sure to get bumped off?" he asked curiously.

"Sure. They ain't a chance of nothin' else. That's where you got the luck. You'll do things that'll start folks talkin' and you'll die while they're still talkin'!"

"Seems to me," said Cadigan, "that a gent might as well do somethin' and then sit down and think about it for the tail end of his life."

[illegible]

you, Danny, because I know that you'd have your tongue cut out before you'd go talkin' about me to other folks. But I tell you that I never worked happy till I had somebody who could watch what I was doin' and talk about it afterward. There was a dozen times when I was sheriff when I could of gone straight after a gang of crooks. But I didn't do it. Because why? Because I didn't love danger, the way you do!"

"Me?" murmured Cadigan. "I don't love it! Love danger? I never heard of such a thing as a gent lovin' danger."

"It's a mighty wise man that knows what he's made of or why he does things. It's a mighty wise man, old son. Love of danger—well, it ain't so doggone uncommon, at that. It ain't common like love of booze, but it turns a gent just as crazy. Look at them gents that start gun fightin' and stay with it? I wasn't one of them kind. Pretty soon I felt my hand gettin' sort of shaky. Then I crawled off up here and got all by myself. Huntin' the copper? The devil, man, I ain't doin' nothin' but occupyin' my mind and tryin' to keep from thinkin' of the doggone coward I was to run away!"

He lifted up his thin face with a sigh, and his small eyes under their wrinkled lids looked over the heads of the great pines and on and on to the huge stone foreheads of the mountains, all pressed against the tender blue of the sky.

"Even if what you say about yourself is true," murmured Cadigan, struck with awe, "what difference does it make? Suppose that you just wanted to look big in front of other folks? Well, Uncle Joe, you got what you want. They all say that you're the bravest, the cleanest, the fastest, the straightest-shootin' gent that ever wore guns in the mountains."

A gleam of joy darted into the eyes of Uncle Joe Loftus like reflected light, and he clasped his bony hands together, trembling from head to foot. Still, he shook his head slowly as he answered Cadigan.

"It ain't no use. I know. You can cheat some folks or most of the folks while you're livin'. But after you're dead, then the truth comes sneakin' out and goes around whisperin' in the ears of folks. And they begin to cuss you first, and then they begin to forget you—and, Cadigan, what a devil of a long time a gent is dead compared to the mite of a time that he's alive! And now how can bein' praised for a minute compare with bein' plumb forgot for a hundred years?"

He went on drearily: "No, sir, I thought about myself, and not about my work. I thought about the advertisin' that I was givin' myself, and not about the help that I was givin' to the law. But them that love their work—why, they talk about what I've done because I'm still alive, but when I'm dead, what I've done'll die with me. But them that love their work, they do bigger things than they know about. And them that love danger—" He fell into a long, gloomy pause.

"Them that love danger?" prompted Cadigan gently. "Who are they?"

"Why, them that go explorin' up into the north pole, and thereabouts. Is it to find something worth while? No, sir. They ain't nothin' there but ice and snow. They tell you that they go for a purpose. No, sir, they ain't got no purpose except to find danger. Every time they start, they're takin' a chance with their life. And it's because of the chance that they go explorin'. They like to roll the dice for the big stakes. Y'understand? And you're like 'em. You're follerin Bill Lancaster. Why?"

"Because he used a gun when I was fightin' only with my fists, Uncle Joe."

"Nope. That ain't it. You're gunna foller him because he's mighty dangerous. And, some day, maybe you'll get him; maybe he'll get you. But if you win, you'll look around for something else that's just as hard to do, and

[illegible]

and rode slowly down the slope. When he looked back he saw the old prospector issuing from the cabin with a pick over his shoulder and a hammer in his hand, his felt hat setting far back on his head, setting out once more on his quest for the hidden lead of copper.

9

CADIGAN'S TIMELY ARRIVAL

One could not imagine William Prentis Lancaster—as his mother had baptized him—being anything other than the center of every scene in which he chose to show himself. Now, while the pig face of Sam Boswick flushed and wrinkled with rage and his huge muscles worked along his arms, and while "Duds" Malone and even Ches Morgan raised their voices in the debate, Bill Lancaster, sitting quietly at the window, was made the more prominent and the more instantly appealing to the eye by his very calm. If he had thundered loud enough to quell them all with his organ tones, he could not have been so thoroughly the most important item in the argument.

But, in the meantime, he chose to stare out the window, idly, as though this matter were entirely beneath his notice, and as though he were interested only in the black-green foresting of conifers which stood thick upon the hills around the town of Gorman. Over this he ran his eyes and noted how the fringes of trees on the rims of the hills pricked roughly against the sky, and how the white rush of the little creek hurtled down the slope, and how, beside the creek, the trail dipped into view and out again behind the trees until the creek itself flattened and widened into a soft-flowing, noiseless stream that ran through the very heart of Gorman and right under the

banks, but even this action picture did not touch deeper than the surface of Lancaster's mind. For he was giving his whole attention to the debate in the room.

The substance of it was that Sam Boswick, who had traveled clear to Kansas City, to secure information on account of which they had been able to rob the P. & S. O. railroad train and come away with a clear twenty-five thousand dollars in profit, declared that he had put in treble or at least double duty upon this ocasion and that he was accordingly due to receive at least two shares instead of one. The objections of Ches Morgan and dapper young Duds Malone were that each of them, in the past, had upon occasion taken more than his share of responsibility and of risk during various of their exploits together, but they had never received an extra share of the money when it was allotted.

Their contentions angered Sam Boswick until he literally swelled with rage. He was one of those immensely powerful men who are usually found in circuses or sometimes in the vaudeville where they hold pianos suspended by straps which are gripped by their teeth alone! Or they lift huge leaden weights, or they support a tangle of eight or ten grown men. They are not always very large. Their muscles in repose look like loose fat. Their muscles in action cover their bodies with rigid knots of iron strength. And such was Sam Boswick. He had the face of a pig and a mind distinguished only for that sort of animal cunning which lives by tricks. But his impulses were so headlong and so steadfast and his might of hand was so great, and withal his bulky muscles could act with such astonishing speed, that he was known and dreaded for a thousand miles. Of the others, Bill Lancaster has already been described. Duds Malone was sufficiently described by his name—he was a slender youth with a pair of big brown eyes and a smile which made the hearts of girls tremble, and he dressed himself as gayly as a Mexican caballero; but the true organizer of the trio, the brains out of which their most profitable exploits nearly aways sprang, was Ches Morgan, who had once been as honest as any man in the mountains until an unfortunate slip of justice had turned him wrong. Ches was driven into outlawry, and there he got the taste of the wild blood and loved it. He still looked as he had always looked, a grave-faced man with tired eyes and hair thickly sprinkled with silver. He had a rough, slow voice, and his pipe was constantly between his teeth. He had even been known to puff slowly at it while he drilled away with his rifle at a distant target—and a human target at that! It was Ches who put the case most strongly, and finally became the spokesman entirely for both himself and Duds Malone.

"Who asked you to go?" he said. "You said you was ready to take the trip and that you figgered that you could do pretty well in Kansas City. You knowed some folks there. If I'd been in your boots I'd of done the same thing. Why, Sam, when we all come out of Juarez on the jump that time in Augusta and they shot your hoss right out from under you, and I pulled up and give you a lift until we hit the river—I say, after I done that, did I ask for a double share for what I'd done for you?"

"I've heard about that a long time," declared Sam Boswick harshly. "But ain't I paid you double for that a couple of times, Morgan?"

"How come?"

"Ain't I backed you up three times when you was busted at poker?"

"Can money pay for them things, Sam?"

"Money can pay me for what *I* done," said Sam bitterly, "and maybe that's where the difference is!"

"Money," said Ches Morgan coldly, "ain't a particular good thing to live for."

"Maybe this here is a church or a Sunday school, or something like that?" grunted Mr. Boswick. "All I want

[illegible]

and almost with an air of pity, so disinterested was his expression.

"I don't call no names," said Morgan calmly. "When it comes to that sort of talk, I let my guns speak for me. Well, Boswick, it looks like you ain't gunna be satisfied until you get a share as big as the chief gets."

This shifted the center of attention sharply toward Lancaster who, however, paid no heed to them.

"Look here, now," went on Boswick, lowering his voice. "They ain't no need to bring Lancaster into this here fix. You know and I know that Lancaster ain't done nothin' for us except hang around. He ain't taken no share in nothin'. He's played safe and held back. He ain't even knowed enough to give orders. He ain't nothin' more'n a figgerhead, partner, and you know it! The main thing we got him for," he continued, even more boldly as the vacant eye of Lancaster, fixed upon the woodland beyond the window, betrayed no consciousness of the conversation which was proceeding so close to him, "the main thing we got him for was to keep us all hangin' together and keepin' the traces tight. But doggone me if he's been able to do even that! I ask you, free and frequent, partner, what right has the captain—if you want to call him that—got to a double share?"

"Ask him!" broke in Duds Malone with a wicked little smile.

Sam Boswick started. Bold and bad as he felt himself

to be, it was plain that he had no desire to array himself against the taller man in single combat.

"Leave it up to Lancaster, this double share of yours," said Ches Morgan. "Maybe he can make it come out straight for you!"

"Well, old son, I'll try!" muttered Boswick, and he turned sharply upon Lancaster.

"Say, Bill!" he called.

The ear of Lancaster caught that voice well enough. As a matter of fact, he had been straining his attention for some time to make out everything that had been said in the room, and he had succeeded fairly well in spite of his abstracted expression and his half-turned back. But now, at the very moment when he was called, he was beginning to center a considerable portion of his attention upon a horseman whom he had been watching as the latter wound down the trail through the evergreens. It was at this moment that the rider turned out from the narrow trail onto the broader, rutted road and jogged his bird-headed, ugly mustang straight for the town. Here Lancaster straightened with a start and a glimmer of cruel joy appeared in his eyes, for the odd familiarity of the stranger had clicked home in his mind, at the last. It was Cadigan, come within his reach at last. After these months of careful inquiry, after the hundreds of miles which he had ridden in search of the younger fellow, here was Cadigan at last come blindly home to him! Lancaster felt all the anger which had been roused in his breast by what he had overheard of the speeches of Boswick, disappear in a trice, and his mind was smoothed. Cadigan was his at last!

How much it meant, not one of the others could understand. Therefore he did not speak of it. But how much it meant to Lancaster could be comprehended by the fact that every one of the hardy three whto were in the room with him would instantly have recognized that name.

The reason was that the entire cattle range and the whole lumbering and mining districts, wherever the famous name of Lancaster was familiarly spoken of, there the name of Cadigan was known also. For, just as the unknown four rounder becomes celebrated overnight because he has fought a drawn battle with the champion of champions, so the man who had stood up to terrible Bill Lancaster and struck him the first blow—the man who had [illegible]

most convenient disappearance of the young waddie.

In the meantime, Lancaster had been constrained to support his reputation by touring around the range ceaselessly letting all men see that he was ready and willing to meet the man he hated and whom it was so falsely said he had wronged. This boldness helped him a great deal and bolstered his falling reputation. But nothing could make up for the disappearance of Cadigan entirely. He had either been murdered, or else he had gone away for a purpose, and when he appeared again he would make himself felt at once. Such was the general opinion. As for the meeting between Cadigan and Lancaster, it was never reported correctly. Even the cow-punchers who had witnessed the thing were not able to converse about it in agreement with one another. For, after all, the whole matter had been excessively simple. Only the change in Cadigan himself had been so remarkable. He had swelled to a new stature in the fight.

And, telling of the battle, they could not help concentrate upon Cadigan. They could not help speaking as though what he had done were really far more remarkable than the facts of the matter.

Such was the way in which the battle between Cadigan and Bill Lancaster had been noised abroad, making the name of the former as much a household word as was the latter. And therefore it was that Lancaster grinned with delight as he saw his foeman, grinned like a cat when it is about to leap on the bird, a smile full of blood hunger, without mirth.

He turned, then, to Sam Boswick as the latter repeated his question for the third time with some irritation.

"Look here, Lancaster, I wish that you'd tell me what *you* think is the right way out of this here. Do I get two shares or not?"

"Why," said Lancaster, "did you ever get two shares before this here?"

"Nope."

"When you started off for Kansas City, did you tell the boys that you wouldn't make the trip and try to use your friends in this here game unless you got a double share?"

"I dunno that I said just that," said the pig-faced man gloomily.

"Well," said Lancaster, "it looks to me like a gent that breaks the laws of the gang, or tries to break the laws of the gang, had ought to get punished in some way. What have we got to do to make Boswick know that we ain't to be fooled with?"

"Punished?" thundered Boswick. "Me?" And he swelled like a poisoned toad until the buttons of his vest creaked against the cloth, so wild was he with his fury.

"I said punished," said Lancaster grimly. "But maybe they's two things that'll help to let you off. The first is that before today you gents ain't ever thought of punishments for them that busted the rules of the gang; the second is that *you* have worked mighty hard at this here game. Well, old son, I dunno but what you're pretty lucky to get off!"

"And the extra share?" muttered big Boswick, rather awed in spite of himself.

"D'you take us for fools, Sam?" roared Lancaster.

Boswick swayed a little from side to side, like a bull about to charge, but charge he did not. The red flag of insult had been waved in his eyes, but at the last instant a thought like a bullet passed through his brain that he was about to seek trouble with the most dexterous gun fighter in the mountains. So he paused, breathing hard. Lancaster, as if to show how little he considered the quarrel or the strength of his recent judgment, turned toward the window.

"Look out at the young gent ridin' by," he said. "You've all heard of him, I reckon. See if you know his face!"

[illegible]

And the youth, hearing his name mentioned by several voices at once, looked up to the window and saw three men looking down at him with a peering interest. And behind them, in the shadow, was a gloomier countenance half lost in the obscurity. Lancaster!

10

"SORT OF DUMB AND SIMPLE!"

It was a pleasant and a timely interruption for the men in the hotel. Sam Boswick, thinking matters over very seriously, felt that he had taken too many liberties with the mighty reputation and the still mightier facts of Lancaster's prowess. He wanted an opportunity for retreat. He wanted to give up his own defiant position as gracefully as possible, and this little interim, so thoughtfully furnished by the newly chosen captain of the trio, gave him the needed pause during which he could readjust himself to the situation. And, after all, it was perhaps better, he decided, that the new captain should have his way. During the brief year through which the three of them had tried to work together, they had recognized the powers of one another and the possibilities of their cooperation. Duds Malone had the invention and the daring of the devil himself; Ches Morgan was a gun fighter second in lightning skill and accuracy only to Duds Malone himself and fortified with a great deal of knowledge of the mountain-desert, both the people and their ways, to say nothing of the country in which they lived. As for Sam Boswick, he had his own type of courage and of brute cunning, which often succeeded even in important matters like the train robbery; he had, besides, a convenient gift—the immense power of his hands! But, with all of these interlocking gifts,

[illegible]

window. Then all four recoiled, with exclamations from the three followers of Lancaster.

"Why," said Ches Morgan, summing up the opinion of them all: "He ain't no more'n a kid! You could tie him in a knot with one hand and spank him with the other, old-timer!"

Lancaster merely shrugged his shoulders. He said graciously: "I ain't got any bad grudge agin' that kid. He's lied a lot about what he's done to me, but then he has brains. And I admire a gent with brains. The way he dropped out of sight and hid himself so's nobody could find him sure enough was smart. You got to admit that, boys! If it wasn't that they's been so much talk, I could let him off, but the way it is, doggoned if I don't have to kill him. You see for yourself how it is. If I didn't salt him away, they's some folks that'd never stop talkin' about me pretty scandalous!"

This speech he uttered with a sort of sad gravity, as a statesman might regret an unfortunate necessity of public interest which called for the head of a political rival. The others, however, voted down his proposal and drowned him with noise. It was Duds Malone who spoke first, joyous as a mischievous fox when it sees a goose far from water and with clipped wings.

"I'll take this here Cadigan," he announced happily. "This here is a job that I'd ought to do. He ain't worth your attention, chief. Why, darned if he don't look like a mama's boy! He ain't finished bein' coddled, hardly!"

The voice of big Sam Boswick rolled heavily in upon him: "What elected you for this here party, young feller? I'll take this Cadigan on and finish him up brown. It ain't gun work that he needs. Any fool could see that guns ain't what he would be hard to clean up with. What the story says is that he's stood up to Bill, here, with his bare hands, and started to give Bill a trimmin' that way until—"

Ches Morgan, clearing his throat violently, recalled Sam to himself and he desisted.

"I'll match you," said Duds, "to see who gets the first crack at him. That is, if the chief will let us have a crack at him at all. He's Lancaster's meat, of course, but I'd like to have a hand at him first."

In spite of the overbearing nature of Lancaster, he was a wise and politic man. And while he was willing to risk himself mightily, he had no desire to throw himself away when another was willing to be the sacrifice. Besides, if a lesser man than himself—if a man like Boswick or like Malone—disposed of Cadigan, it would make the importance of that youth disappear, whereas if he were destroyed by Lancaster himself, the youngster might remain much of a hero in the eyes of many men. There was another thing which prevailed upon Lancaster. He remembered the odd change which had come over the face and the eyes of Cadigan when he rose from the bunk to fight on that historic occasion not many months before. It still made the blood of Lancaster run cold to think of it.

He said quietly: "If you boys want your fun, I ain't standin' in your way. Toss a coin to see who takes the party."

The coin was tossed. It winked in the air.

"Heads!" called Malone.

But, when it spatted in the palm of Ches Morgan, tails were uppermost; Boswick had gained the first right against young Dan Cadigan. He clamped his sombrero on his head with a grin and shrugged his heavy shoulders.

"Besides," said Boswick, grinning, "I need a mite of exercise, and punchin' a bag is kind of tiresome!" So he made his exit, swaggering a little.

In the meantime, Cadigan had put up his horse in the stable behind the hotel and entered the building itself. On the register, scrawled heavily with clumsy writing, he drew out his own name.

"Daniel Cadigan—" spelled the proprietor, adjusting his glasses and reaching for the key of the room at the [illegible]

dozen loungers who were in the room. They had stiffened in their chairs near the stove, for it was a raw autumn day. They no longer watched the steam rising from their trousers as they dried, or the frost thickening upon the windowpanes. The battery of their eyes turned steadily upon the newcomer.

"You're Cadigan!" gasped out the host again. "Why, Lancaster is—" He paused, anxious lest he should be betraying secrets.

"Lancaster aims to be right here in this hotel, don't he?" said Cadigan.

"Why—" began the host, tortured with curiosity and with fear combined.

"That's why I came," said Cadigan.

They were all on their feet, by this time, watching the man who dared to hunt down Bill Lancaster. They saw a man with the thick neck and the deep chest of a mine laborer, but with long arms and with long, slender hands and feet. Ordinarily they would have given him only a casual glance and put him down as a fellow of stodgy build. But what they knew of him made them examine him with more care, and what they saw meant to them, plainly, speed of hand and speed of foot, plus more than common power.

And when he went up the stairs with the proprietor, their tongues were loosed behind him. Cadigan heard the beginning of their murmuring gossip. But he paid little attention to it. He was too busy wondering at the manner of the host which told him that he was a marked man, and a man marked for great and respectful attention. All of this was a new mode of treatment to Cadigan. He was accustomed to careless words flung over the shoulder to him like bones flung to a dog to keep it quiet.

He was brought to the best room in the house saving that one which was already occupied by Lancaster and his companions. The proprietor busied himself opening a window and moving the chair aimlessly about in an effort to make his guest more comfortable. In the meantime, he was fairly swelling with words which finally burst out.

"Are you really come along here to—to get—Lancaster?" He uttered the last word as one might have uttered the name of an angel, or a fiend. And he found that Cadigan was regarding him mildly, with a faint smile upon his lips—not a secretive expresson, but rather the smile of a happy child.

"I dunno," said Cadigan. "I just dropped in to talk things over with him."

"They ain't gunna be a fight, then?" said the proprietor, fairly aching with disappointment.

"I guess not. I hope—" said Cadigan. "All I want out of him is an explanation how he—"

"An explanation!" bellowed the proprietor. "Out of Lancaster?"

"Sure. Of how come that he forgot himself and used a gun on me when—"

The host backed toward the door with awe and some terror in his eyes. "You might drop in on Mr. Lancaster," said Cadigan, "and tell him that I'd like to have a chat with him—when he's got time!"

The host issued hastily through the door and fled down the hall; on the way he encountered an iron hand which brought him up short. It was that Hercules among men—Sam Boswick, his fleshy brow now gathered in darkness.

"Where's the room where you put up that young skunk, that Cadigan?" he inquired harshly.

"Third door right down the hall. But what—"

"He's been spreadin' a lot of talk about me," muttered the other, and strode on down the hallway.

The host cast one glance of agonized curiosity behind him, saw the door to the bedroom opened and shut behind Boswick, and then rushed on to inform the curious who [illegible]

of combat. Already they could hear the bull voice of Mr. Boswick.

11

BOSWICK GOES AFTER CADIGAN

When Boswick entered the room, he found before him a figure even less imposing than that which had passed under the hotel window a few moments before, for a seat in the saddle, even on a most inadequate horse, is sure to lend a certain dignity to a man. It was a handsome face, in a boyish way, and the eyes of a boy, too, dim and gentle, looked out at him from it. But Sam Boswick never wasted much time and attention upon faces. He had to do with the might of hand and arm, and that might be looked for now in Cadigan. But the big, round throat of Cadigan looked soft and smooth—far other than the heavily corded neck of Boswick. And the shoulders of Cadigan were not ornamented with bulky knots of muscles like the shoulders of Boswick. Moreover, the seal of strength is placed upon the foreheads of mighty men; it sat upon the bull front of Boswick, but in Cadigan it did not appear.

For these reasons, whatever of suspense had remained in the mind of Boswick—remembering that, after all, this man had actually dared to stand up to Lancaster hand to hand—that suspense was now dissipated and a broad grin of brutal contempt formed upon the mouth of the bully. As for that other and famous encounter with Lancaster, it had been accomplished, beyond a doubt, only through the [illegible]

"You ain't?" murmured Cadigan. "Well, I'm mighty sorry to hear that!"

It staggered Boswick, in spite of the low estimate which he had already formed of the other. But such downright "crawling" as this was beneath all imagining! Some of his astonishment and his scorn showed in his face; he made no effort to repress it. But Cadigan seemed unable to read it. He remained standing, waiting for the other to sit down comfortably, waiting to hear this first rude remark explained in more detail with a faintly apologetic smile upon his face and his head canted a little to one side. He reminded Boswick of a faithful dog which has heard a stern word from the master and only hopes that it will not be followed by a blow.

"What I've heard," said Boswick, "is that you're a doggone slick liar, Cadigan."

Cadigan shook his head and frowned, rather in bewilderment than in anger. "I dunno that I ever done much lyin'," he said quietly. "I hope you don't mean that, mister—"

"My name is Boswick," said the man of might.

"Boswick?" repeated Cadigan. "Boswick?" Then he started a little. "It aint likely that you're *Sam* Boswick?"

"That's me," said Boswick, his pride touched deeply.

"The Sam Boswick that lifted the sack of junk iron onto the scales in Tucson when—"

"I done that little trick," said Boswick.

"Why," said Cadigan with a happy smile, "I'm mighty

glad to meet you, Mr. Boswick!" And he advanced with an outstretched hand. The motion was so genuine that Boswick almost stretched out his own hand to meet that of the younger man. But he recollected himself in time and folded his arms sternly.

"I ain't shakin' hands," he said, "till I get the straight of this here matter." He paused and cleared his throat.

"I'll be glad to explain," volunteered Cadigan. "I'm sure that there's some mistake, Mr. Boswick."

"H'm!" growled out the Hercules. "You ain't the Cadigan, then, that's been goin' around the country tellin' folks that you licked Lancaster—Bill Lancaster? Except that he done a dirty trick—"

"Oh," said Cadigan amiably. "I never told nobody that I licked Lancaster."

"You didn't?"

"They didn't seem to need tellin'. They seemed to know."

Boswick roared suddenly: "Are you sayin' that to my face?" For he was glad to have something on which to base his wrath.

"It's true," said Cadigan.

"Look here, Cadigan. Lancaster is a friend of mine."

"I'm mighty sorry to hear that."

"And I'm here to tell you that if you say you done up Lancaster—you lie, Cadigan." He added, when Cadigan merely blinked at him: "You hear me? I say you lie!"

"It looks to me," said Cadigan, "like you come here huntin' trouble with me."

"I ain't ever turned my back on a fight, son. Can you say that much?"

And Cadigan walked to the door of his room. "Would you mind steppin' out into the hall with me, Mr. Boswick?"

"I can talk plenty right here, son!"

"You see," said Cadigan, "by my way of bringing' up, it ain't right to fight a gent in your own house—or your own room."

Mr. Boswick looked upon him with utter amazement. This, to be sure, was a novel way of avoiding trouble. He could hardly believe his ears, and he stared dubiously at the other. What he saw was a strange transformation taking place in Cadigan. It seemed to him that the other was growing inches taller and that his whole body had expanded. But the greatest change was in his face. It [illegible]

Then Cadigan waded in and drove his fist into the ribs of the larger man.

It seemed to Boswick that his whole side caved in. It was like the falling of a wall against him, squeezing out his breath as from a collapsed bellows. Then two arms went around him; closed about him like red-hot steel being shrunk into place. Boswick tore at those grappling arms. It was like tearing at two ribs of rock and trying to pluck them from the side of a mountain.

Still the pressure continued, greater and greater. His very back seemed breaking. And Boswick, frantic with fear, hurled himself toward the floor. He merely succeeded in giving up his footing, for he found himself heaved into the air, lightly. The door was kicked open, and he was cast into the hall like a stone from a sling.

He lay where he fell, more appalled in spirit than broken in body. Above him leaned the conqueror. His fingers twisted into the hair of Boswick's head and twisted his face up cruelly to the light.

"Did Lancaster send you?" asked Cadigan.

"No—yes!" groaned out Boswick.

"Good!" said Cadigan. "If you'd come on your own account—I'd of broke you in two and throwed the halves away. But now—you go tell Lancaster that I'm waitin' for him. Understand?"

So, with one hand, he raised Boswick to his feet and flung him down the hall.

And Boswick, passing the stairs, saw it crowded with

horrified, astounded faces. That moment repaid Boswick for all the pain which he had given others. For all the shame which he had inflicted on other men, now shame was equally heaped upon his own head. And in the agony of it, he bowed his face and rushed on into the room where Lancaster and Ches Morgan and Duds Malone were waiting for him.

He flung himself into a chair and leaned over the center table, his face buried in his hands, groaning.

"What's up?" cried Malone.

"He's a devil!" gasped out poor Boswick. "He—he's ten men rolled into one! Duds, keep clear of him!"

"Keep clear of him, Duds," echoed Lancaster scornfully. "I don't need no help to fight my own fights. You boys stay here and take it easy. I'll go out and—"

He was distinctly uncomfortable, but there was nothing else for him to do. Certainly, when he dealt with this strange youth a second time, there would be nothing but gun play between them, and the devil take the slower man!

There was a groan from Boswick as he shifted in his chair and raised his stricken face. "He's busted every bone in my body. And he's chain lightnin', Duds. He moves quicker'n a flash of light and hits harder'n a ton of stone fallin' a mile onto your head!"

Duds Malone loosened the bandanna about his throat and then turned to Lancaster. "You stay here," he cautioned. "I tossed a coin for this here chance, and I aim to take it. Lancaster, that gent may be able to hit harder'n Boswick, though it don't seem no ways possible, but if he knows how to handle a gun, then I ain't got any eyes in my head for tellin' a fightin' man!"

He strode from the room, slammed the door behind him, and at the head of the stairs looked down to a jumble of men standing on the landing and in the lobby below.

"Where's Cadigan?" asked Malone of them.

"Cadigan? He's just gone outside—what might you be wantin' of him?" asked the proprietor.

"I'm gunna ask a question," said Malone gayly, tilting

his hat farther back on his head, "that Sam Boswick didn't have a chance to put."

And he passed down the stairs, across the lobby, and out into the sunshine of the afternoon.

12

"BARNEY"

Cadigan went first to the general merchandise store. Through the window the amiable Mr. Duds Malone saw the other purchasing forty-five-caliber cartridges at the famous old worn counter where so many bullets and lives had been bought and sold. And as Mr. Cadigan stuffed the cartridges one by one into his cartridge belt, Mr. Malone heard him whistling softly to himself a foolish song of the range:

"He's a killer and a hater!
He's the great annihilater!
He's the terror of the boundless prairie.

"I'm the snoozer from the upper trail;
I'm the reveler in murder and in gore!
I can bust more Pullman coaches on the rail
Than any one who's worked the job before.

"He's a snorter and a snoozer;
He's the great trunk-line abuser—"

The whistle died, and Cadigan turned to saunter from the store again while Duds Malone shrank around the corner of the building. There was something so genial and

[illegible]

fellow whom he would have picked out as an eminent booby—a most unmanly man, indeed. But there was a tale to the effect that this same fellow had beaten no less a person than Bill Lancaster. Nay, it was beyond a doubt that only a few moments before this same man had encountered with that Hercules among men, Sam Boswick, and had crumpled him as though he were no more than a child. For these reasons, Mr. Malone slipped into the background and watched Cadigan step out into the sunshine again.

He took off his hat to it and stood with his head raised as though he were enjoying every scruple of the warmth on this autumn day. Duds Malone studied him with keenest interest. As for the physical power of the man, he could understand that after seeing him move. For in spite of his solid build his step was light and easy. Hidden in those smooth shoulders there might be the strength of an ox and the speed of a striking rattler. Duds Malone thought it very probable that there was! He regarded the body less than the face. And he decided that Cadigan's countenance was not exactly dull—only simple. There was no more artifice or malice in that face than in a crystal pool. It was full of a placid innocence like that which poets affect to see in beautiful girls and for which other men strain their eyes in vain. And Malone was tempted, indeed, to call it a very handsome face—except that it was a little too full and sleek—except for that very placidity of expression. Indeed, all the component parts of a fine manhood appeared in Cadigan except fire. And fire in him there was none apparent on the surface, no matter what a blaze of spirit might be concealed in him. Mr. Duds Malone was a thoughtful man, and it appeared to him that, in the person of Cadigan, there was plenty to exercise all of his mind. Cadigan began to stroll aimlessly down the street which wound and twisted among the shacks which made up Gorman. It never seemed that Gorman had grown up along the trail; it rather seemed that the roadway had been hastily and rudely constructed through the midst of Gorman. By dint of building on at either end, Gorman had been drawn out to an absurd length; and it would have no thickness at all, had it not been for the snaky course of the main street. Along this roadway proceeded Cadigan, and Duds Malone came behind him, as secret as a spirit of the night. And every moment that he followed the stranger the greater grew his doubts of himself and the probable outcome of the battle when they joined together in fight. It was the serenity of Cadigan which was impressing him more, at every moment. It had seemed at first that it was the complacence of a fool; now it began to seem to Duds Malone the calm indifference of a most extraordinary man to whom dangers are nothing and victories are taken as a matter of course.

Such was the decision which was forming in the mind of Duds Malone when, without warning, Mr. Cadigan turned abruptly to the side and passed down a little alley lined with young spruce trees on either side—beautiful silver spruces, the king of trees. Duds Malone followed, taking skillful shelter behind the trunks and with an odd lifting of the heart. In all Gorman this was the walk most familiar to him, for at the end of the little by-street was the Morris cottage in which lived Louise—the others didn't matter. A month before Duds had proposed to her for the fifth time and been for the fifth time rejected. Yet they were friends still. Sometimes Duds attributed this fact to the strength of his passion. Sometimes he felt that it was due to the singular tact of Lou. But he was at least sure that if he could not win her no one else could, which after all was a precarious comfort.

He heard the voice of Lou's brother, Richard Morris, shouting in the distance.

"Here, Barney! Here, boy! Darn the fool! He ain't got

[illegible]

veritable giant among dogs. He had the imposing build of a Great Dane together with a brown and white coat, like that of a Saint Bernard; withal, his pricking, sharp-pointed ears gave him something of the air of a wolf, and savage as any wolf's was the growl of defiance which rumbled out of his throat.

"Come here, or I'll brain you!" yelled big Richard Morris.

"That's no way," said his sister with much disapproval. "That's no way to try to handle him, Rickie."

"Lemme alone, will you?" thundered Richard. "The dog's a plain fool!"

He heaved at the rope again, and suddenly Barney gave way to the strain. Or rather, the annoyance became too much for him, and he charged straight at his master. One would have expected a lumbering action in such a mountain of dog flesh, but the great boar-hound body of Barney had not been given to him for nothing. As a wolf slides frictionlessly along, with deceptive speed, so moved Barney, driving close to the ground, a brown streak dashed with white. And Cadigan, pausing close to the fence, saw the great mouth strain open inside the heavy wire muzzle, saw the lips curl back from glistening fangs; and then the monster leaped.

Beside Richard on the ground, reserved for just such an emergency as this, was a wooden bludgeon of ample dimensions, ending in a knotty head. This, as Barney charged, he had caught up and now he struck with all his might;

it would have cracked a skull even as strong as that of the big dog had it landed fairly on his head. But Barney had swerved in the very act of leaping, so that the blow merely bounced off the thick, rubbery padding of muscles along his shoulder. He had aimed at the throat, and the muzzle struck fairly on his target; then the weight of that driving body catapulted Richard head over heels.

The shock flung Barney into the air. Behold! He twisted over like a cat and landed on his feet while the scream of the girl tingled in the air; Cadigan leaped over the fence. He saw Richard roll to a sitting posture with crimson streaming from a cut mouth and with a revolver in his hand.

"I'll kill the murderin' fool!" yelled Rickie.

"No, no!" screamed the girl. "He's helpless—he can't hurt you with that muzzle on and—"

Cadigan scooped up the end of the fallen rope, and as Barney charged again, he dug his heels into the ground and planted his weight, yelling at the same time: "Don't shoot!"

The revolver balanced in the ready hand of Richard Morris; but if he pressed the trigger, yonder was the stranger in line with him and the dog. If the bullet went astray it might mean the death of a man, not a mere dumb brute. So the trigger finger of Richard was stayed. Then big Barney reached the end of the rope.

It was most unfair. With such a length of line a dexterous cow-puncher can stop a running horse; and at the farther end this rope was anchored by a hundred and ninety pounds of such muscle as had never stepped into the town of Gorman before this day. There could be only one conclusion. Barney was flipped upon his back with stunning force. He rolled to his feet instinctively, but there he stood snarling faintly, his legs braced, waiting for his wits to return like a stunned boxer in the prize ring—"out on his feet."

"Stand back from him!" cried Richard. "Get out of the way, stranger. I'm through with that dog. I'm done with him!"

He poised his revolver for the coup de grâce, but Cadigan did not jump to the side. He merely began to hand in the rope while he walked quickly up to the big dog as it stood swaying slightly from side to side. Then Louise reached the place of action. She leaped in before her big brother and confronted him with her head thrown back and

[illegible]

is it me?"

"You've clubbed him and jerked him around until you could have driven anything fighting mad, let alone a wild dog like Barney."

"Ain't I had him two months? Ain't I worked with him every day since then?"

"But Rickie, hasn't he run wild all his life? Hasn't he hunted with wolves and—"

"Nope. But he's *hunted* wolves!"

"He's lived like a wild beast—with his wits and his teeth. D'you think that you can tame him in a minute?"

"Two months ain't a minute, Lou. You're talkin' foolish, I tell you?"

"Two months?" She snapped her fingers. "Why, Rickie, the scars of the trap you caught him in are still there on his leg. They're hardly healed!"

"Maybe so," grumbled Rickie, touching his hand to his bleeding mouth, "but I'm tired of this blockhead. He ain't fit to live! He's got no sense at all!"

"Give him to me, Rickie."

"I ain't gunna have him around the house. Besides, I'm gunna teach him sense. I'm gunna—"

"Teach him by killin' him? Rickie, dear Rickie, let me have Barney!"

"Not in a million years!"

"Wait and try to sell him, then!"

"Nobody but a fool would pay ten dollars for him. Not if they knowed what Barney is."

"Look!" whispered the girl. She pointed past Rickie, who turned with her to view a most strange tableau of the huge brown dog standing with his head cocked curiously to one side staring up to the face of Cadigan.

"He *knows* him!" gasped out Lou, clasping her hands together in amazement.

"Knows a wolf? Don't talk foolish!" But even as he spoke, his voice lowered to somethng of respect and awe at the very thought.

13

WITHOUT GUN OR CLUB

There was far more to be read in Cadigan, however, than in the big brute before him. There was a sort of hungry wistfulness stamped in his eyes and quivering in his face, drawing all his features more tense, refining them. He did not draw his glance from the big dog as he said:

"Speakin' of buyin' this dog—I got ten dollars that ain't workin', partner."

The glances of the girl and her brother flashed together and held on one another, as though they were exchanging thoughts. Then they separated again and turned back to Cadigan.

"Speakin' of buyin'," said Richard, "I dunno that I want to sell."

"Why not?" asked Lou suddenly and strongly. "Why not sell Barney, Rickie, if we can't do anything with him—poor Barney!"

At this, Cadigan turned to the girl and saw her for the first time. To be sure, he was not so blind as to have failed to see her form and face before this, but they had been nothing to him more than a pasteboard silhouette might have been. Indeed, no woman was more than that to him. From the days of his boyhood he had not looked with any awareness into the eyes of any woman or girl other than his mother until her death, and Sophie Preston, until he left school. But it seemed to Cadigan, when he turned to Louise Morris on this day of days, that a door opened in his mind and let in a flood of light, and the light was the face of Louise, and all that lay behind her eyes. Hers was a sunburned loveliness. Her cheeks were as brown as her hands, and those slender hands, so delicately made, were as strong as the hands of a boy. Like a boy's, too, was her smile, until one grew aware of the dimple which formed and faded in her right cheek; but her eyes were the eyes of a woman. To Cadigan they were as wonderful as the first sight of an uncharted shore to an explorer.

Some learn by gradual degrees, going forward step by step and adding one to one to make their million; but others stand still almost all their days, only on rare occasions leaping forward—perhaps to a greater distance than the steady plodders ever attain. Cadigan was one of these. All his life had been one long sleep, it might be said, broken by one lightning flash in his boyhood when he had discovered, climbing the windmill beside the school, that he loved danger for its own sake. Now there was another thunderstroke which stunned him and amazed him and opened his whole soul; it was on this day when he turned to Louise. But no one could have guessed it. Not a muscle in his face stirred; only a light glittered for an instant in his eyes and went out again, drawn deep into his heart where it was to glow and make a sad sunshine to the last day of his life. All in a moment, then, Cadigan left this sober earth and stepped far away into a fairyland from which he could never return—a miracle in that dusty back yard; and like most miracles, it was not noticed.

"I ain't had a right chance with Barney," explained Richard sullenly. "I ain't had a chance to learn him and his ways right, and—"

His sister stamped a slim booted foot in her impatience.

"You know as well as I do, Rickie Morris, that you've never gone near him without being snarled at, and look!

I don't think Barney would hurt this man even if his muzzle were off!"

"That's crazy!" answered Rickie, flushing. "I guess I get on with dogs and hosses as well as most. That devil'd

[illegible]

said Rickie Morris, "and then if you got the nerve to take that muzzle off'n him—and if he don't sink his teeth in you—"

"Rickie!" cried his sister, shocked.

"I ain't askin' him to," said Rickie gloomily. "But if he's fool enough to take a chance like that—why, I'll *give* him the dog!"

"You won't try it!" exclaimed the girl to Cadigan, but Cadigan was lost in a contemplation of the great-headed brute which now had squatted on his haunches, staring up in the face of the man.

"I've heard a sayin'," he said, "that every dog knows his master when he sees him."

"But that's not a dog!' cried the girl. "He—he—"

"He's what?" snapped out her brother. "Of course he's a dog. What else could he be? That's the cattle killer that's been raisin' so much trouble down in the Little Pocas Valley, stranger. They ain't no doubt about that. I seen his trail and his sign down there. It's the same one! He's a dog, all right, but he's run wild all his life; he's turned wolf, and he'll stay wolf till he dies, I say!"

There was no doubt that in those big, dark eyes there was intelligence enough to plot the death of the stoutest bull that ever walked the plains, and in the jaws, armed with the immense fangs and equipped with muscles that bulged in huge knots at the side of his head, there was power enough to tear out the throat of horse or cow. Power enough, too, to kill a man with a single crunch!

That was the last thought which darted into the mind of Cadigan; if he took the muzzle off the animal, he would be taking death into his hands. With that, he drew out from beneath his coat that ancient and trusty pair of revolvers which had been donated to him by strange old Uncle Joe Loftus. He handed them in silence to Morris.

"Look here," said the latter, "you ain't—well, darned if it ain't your business—not mine."

Cadigan without a word, stepped back to the huge beast and laid his hand on the buckle which fastened the muzzle. Louise ran close to him, stopped short by the murderous growl of the big dog which shook his whole body, so deep was his fury.

"What do you aim to do?" she cried.

He looked up to her in silence, but with a faint smile on his lips and a faint light in his eyes. Bill Lancaster had once confronted that same light, and he had understood; the girl understood also, and she shuddered. The very power of speech seemed to be taken from her, but as she shrank back, she cast a glance of appeal to her brother.

"He thinks he knows his business," said Rickie savagely. "Let him alone. It ain't our fault—if something happens!"

The hand of Cadigan had no sooner touched the neck of Barney than the great head of the dog lowered a little and his lips curled back from his fangs. Yet Cadigan slipped the strap through the buckle; the growl of Barney was a rumble of distant thunder; and the shiver of battle hunger took hold upon his stalwart body. Louise slipped to the side of her brother and clung to him.

"Steady up, Lou," said Richard through his teeth, though his own brow was covered with perspiration. "Steady up; don't be scared. If anything should start—I could shoot the dog—"

"It's not that," whispered the girl, her fascinated eyes still holding fast to the group before her. "But it's that man—look, Rickie! He seems to be—almost—almost—happy!"

"By the Heavens," exclaimed the youth, "I think he is! Looks like he was opening a package along about Christmas time!"

Now, very softly, Cadigan began to slip the muzzle from

that dreadful head, but at the first movement of the wire cage the brute leaped suddenly back. His head was free! He shook it, as though to make sure that his sense told him the truth. Then he dropped to his belly in the dust

[illegible]

dog considered them as less than nothing. No fur-clothed hide protected the tender throat of this creature. The very tingle of death was already in the fangs of Barney; he was tasting the life of the man.

So Barney began to crawl forward, little by little, his belly in the dust, saliva beginning to run from his jowls, so keenly was he foretasting the life of this man!

"Look, Rickie!" gasped out the girl.

But Rickie had lost the power to shoot. The guns hung limp in his hands at his side and his mouth was agape, and his face was the color of sun-yellowed paper. Barney was crawling closer, and the stranger had not moved!

It was not a question of trying to meet the eye of a dumb brute and conquer it so; Cadigan stayed simply because he could not find it in his heart to flee and because, if he fled, he knew that his first step would bring the monster on his back with a leap. After that, one grip of the huge jaws would break his neck. So Cadigan waited, saying over and over to his hear: "I've done that dog no harm; that dog ain't goin' to harm me!"

Two paces away the forward motion of the monster stopped, and he shrank smaller in the dust, tensing his muscles for the leap. Lou Morris strove to cry out; but her voice died in her throat. Then Barney, with a growl which might have killed by mere terror, suddenly sat erect and stared at the strange thing which refused to either fight or flee.

A voice spoke to him, and at the sound of the human

tongue, he started and crouched again with his fangs bared, but this was not a voice filled with curses and commands; it spoke as from man to man, gently, and a thrill of intolerable wonder and joy leaped through the body of Barney and passed on into his soul.

There was more in the heart of the killer than he himself knew, but as he listened to the voice of the man, the heritage of centuries grew suddenly big in him. The voice went on, softly—so softly that it barely reached the ears of the two who stood at the side, waiting. But to the ear of the brute every breath and accent was underlined with meaning. What meaning?

It was as if a doe which he had worn down on the trail had turned upon him, not to fight desperately to the end, not even in paralyzing fear, but to watch him without curiosity, even, gently, kindly—gently—kindly! Here was a life which was his for the tap of a tooth; but what of the other thing—the flowing voice?

Barney dropped upon his haunches and lifted his head to the sky and a deep wail like the wail of a wolf but deeper, richer, and echoing farther, and poignant with that dreary note which comes out of the wilderness, issued from the throat of the dog and rolled over Gorman, and thundered faintly up the slopes of Gorman Pass.

"By the heavens!" gasped out Morris.

"Hush!" warned the girl. "Don't speak! You'll break the spell!"

The wail died out; there sat the wolf-dog before the man; bristling with rage, snarling and slavering with the fury to kill, trembling, too, with a deathless hunger to escape from these men and these minds of men which strove to imprison his own. He wanted to kill, and he could not; he wanted to flee, and he dared not stir; and the conflict turned Barney into a shuddering, ravening beast from a nightmare world—midnight stepping into midday. But still that voice went on!

And then a hand was stretched forth, palm up, the ancient sign of amity between man and all the rest of the world. Barney shrank down, ready to leap again. But the hand held neither gun nor club, and the voice had not altered.

Still, one could never tell. Barney dropped his head upon his paws. He had the patience of the wolf pack, which waits for the circle of cows at bay to break. He had the patience which looks winter starvation in the face and [illegible]

14

AT THE HEAD OF THE MONSTER

There were four feet from the head of the dog to the man. It took Cadigan one hour to cover that distance, but during that hour Lou Morris and her brother did not stir; and Duds Malone, behind a nearby silver spruce, did not stir; and half a dozen passers-by remained rooted in place to watch. It took a whole hour, but there was never a dull moment. It required a whole hour and left the face of Cadigan drawn and gray with effort, but at the end of that time, while a groan of apprehensive horror came from the bystanders, he actually sat down under the very nose of Barney.

And, Barney, shrinking into perfect position to spring, gaped his mouth wide open. For three seconds Cadigan had one chance in a hundred of living and then—the rumbling growl ceased, and the quiet murmur of the man's voice was audible again. What was he saying, talking so constantly for so long a time? He was talking as if an intelligence behind the eyes of the brute could register his words and conceive an answer to them.

For he said: "Speakin' by and large, Barney, I ain't

loaded up my life with a lot of acquaintances, because you can't always tell by the way gents act whether they're friends or not friends. Y'understand? But by the looks of you, Barney, I aim to figger out what's goin' on inside of

[illegible]

strange scene. At dinner time Lou Morris brought out a dinner to Cadigan, and with the rope drawn close, he reached for the plate and ate its contents, never daring for a half instant to take his gaze from that of the wild dog.

When the dark came and the stars rolled out in shimmering ranks stretched through the sky, Lou came again and sat on the ground not far away. All was dim and dull in the yard, but when her eyes grew accustomed to the light, she saw a strange spectacle of the great battle-front of Barney resting in the lap of the stranger. That formidable head lay across the knees of the man, and between the wolfish, pricking ears of the brute and along his thick mane ran the hand of his master in slow caresses. She spoke, and there was an instant growl of warning from the great brute, which reared his head suddenly and stared at her with eyes glaring green through the night.

"You've tamed him!" she said softly, as the hand and the voice of the man reduced the giant to quiet submission again.

"Tamed him?" said Cadigan slowly. "Tamed him? No, that ain't just it. I guess nobody could do that. Tamin'—that means breakin' him. He ain't like a hoss. You never could use him for nothin' except a sort of a partner."

She pondered this for a long time. "I never thought of that," she said at length. "You know a lot about dogs and horses and things, I guess."

She could see him shake his head. "Not that, Miss

Morris. But like 'em better and I know 'em better'n I do men."

"Oh!" said she. "D'you mean that? But why?"

"Why, they're kinder,' said Cadigan.

She thought of the huge wild dog crawling on his belly toward Cadigan, fairly quivering with murderous zeal to get its teeth in his throat. Kinder? It occurred to her, then, that this man was a quiet jester, full of dry wit, but she had hardly begun to smile when she realized, without a word spoken, that he was probably a man who had never made a jest in his life. That was not his way, and that was not his strength.

"Will he do what you want him to?" she asked afterward.

"I dunno," said Cadigan. "I thought about that. We ain't hardly acquainted, yet."

"Would he follow you?"

He rose to his feet. Behind him the wolf-dog rose also, and slunk in a circle behind Cadigan until the latter returned to his former place and sat down. Instantly Barney dropped beside him and lowered his head in the lap of the man. To the girl, who had seen this beast furious and raging every time a human being approached it, this was a miracle, and nothing else.

But oh, what a joy to make that rough monster submit to the touch of the hand—ay, accept it with joy and with the deep beginning of love!

"Could you make him let me—touch him?" she asked.

"You! No," said Cadigan decidedly, and she was hurt.

"If he'll follow," she said a little more coldly, "why do you still keep him here?"

"Because every minute we stay here, we get a little thicker. He's getting tied to me; I'm getting tied to him, and so, maybe, when we go off together and he comes across a trail of a rabbit or a partridge, he ain't goin' to slide away on it and foller his nose up the wind and leave me alone behind him. And if I stay here alone with him long enough, there ain't gunna come a time when I'll come across another trail and go follerin' the sign of it and leave him here behind me. You understand?"

She drew a breath. "Partly," she said. Then she added afterward: "You are a very gentle man!"

There was such a pause after this that she thought he [illegible]

"Not one?"

"Nary a friend. Well, maybe I got to make one exception."

"Ah, I thought so. Who is it?"

"Barney, here. I aim to think he's a friend of mine already." He said it so simply that she could not help but believe him. But when she tried to comprehend such a thing, her wits failed her. A life without a friend!

"Oh," she added suddenly, "you mean that there's no one you're really fond of—but what *do* you mean by a friend?"

"Some one," said he sadly, "who's glad to see you come and who's sorry to see you go."

It made her fairly dizzy. Every waking moment, well-nigh, she spent among smiles. But to have no one—in all the world—no one!

"Isn't it terribly lonely?" she asked.

"I never thought about it before tonight," said Cadigan. And he added suddenly, with a great breath: "Yes; it's terrible lonely!"

He was talking like a child, just as directly, and just as simply. It unnerved Lou. It was stealing the weapons of women and turning them against their proper owners, this perfect naïveté.

"Why," she said at last, "won't you let me come near Barney? I think you could handle him if he tried to bite me. Besides, Rickie gave you back your guns, didn't he?"

"The nacher of this here dog," said Cadigan gravely,

"seems to be to take a flyer straight for the throat. If I was to miss a shot at him, he wouldn't miss his shot at you. I guess you'd better stay clear of the dog."

"Lou!" called the voice of her mother, as the screen door at the back of the house creaked open.

"Coming, mother!" answered Lou cheerfully. But she made no move to rise. "How long will you stay here with Barney!" she asked.

"I dunno. Till things get quieted down in the town, I guess."

"What'll you do then with him?"

"We'll make a kill, I guess. Barney aims to be hungry, by the way his stomach is tucked up in him. D'you see?"

"Louise!" shouted Mrs. Morris from the distant blackness of the house.

"Coming!" cried Louise. She said to Cadigan: "When you take the trail, do you leave Gorman?"

"I dunno," said Cadigan. "I'm waitin' around here for a man—"

"Do you want work?'

"You might call it work, in a way," said Cadigan softly.

"My dad knows everybody in Gorman Pass," said the girl. "He could get a place for you. I hope you don't go away!"

Cadigan was silent. Indeed, he could not speak, but he told himself that he knew now, without possible doubt, that there were no two ways about it: Lou Morris was an angel of the brightest light!

"You see," went on the girl, "if you go, Barney'll be gone with you. And I'm mighty interested in Barney!"

"Oh," murmured Cadigan.

"And," she said, correcting herself hastily and heartily, "you'd find that you can have a good time hereabouts, you know. We have mighty bang-up dances. You'd ought to hear the orchestra over in the schoolhouse when we have a dance! It's one of the very best. And I've been clean to Denver and heard 'em play there, you know."

"Well," said Cadigan, "you see how it is—I—"

"Louise Morris, are you comin' this minute? Or do I have to send your dad to fetch you?"

"Coming right quick," said Louise, rising tardily to her

knees. Then she sank back upon her heels again. She could not leave this new man, this fascinating stranger, fascinating in his weird difference, compared with all others. Not even pretty Maggie Johnson's wooer from St. Louis was

[illegible]

For after all, Lou Morris was like any other very pretty and very young girl—she knew her strength, and a certain quality in the voice of Cadigan when he spoke in the darkness—a certain reticent gentleness, it might be called—told her that he was hers if she chose to have him. This was a conquest which she would have despised because of its ease, except that women rarely do despise any conquest, no matter how trifling, just as the wild Indians of another day rejoiced almost equally in every scalp—whether it were that a grown man or even an infant. Besides, if Cadigan were a cheap conquest to her, at least he was given significance by what he was in other respects.

"You were saying something," said Louise.

"Why, about dances. I was going to say that—you see, I don't dance, Miss Morris."

"Oh! Don't you? Honest?" She paused to consider this. Because every one dances on the range; it is one of the possible amusements, and therefore every one must join in. "Well," said Lou, "we could teach you. *I* could teach you!"

"Would you do that?" said Cadigan, so simply, but with such a heartfelt gratitude in his voice that it staggered the girl.

"Of course I would!"

"Louise!" thundered a heavy bass voice coming from the direction of the house.

"Coming!" called Louise, jumping to her feet. "That's dad, you know," she explained hastily to Cadigan. "You'll be around to-morrow, won't you? You'll come to see me?"

"Do you want me to?" breathed Cadigan, hardly able to make his voice audible.

"Of course! And I want to see Barney, don't I? By to-morrow you'll be able to do most anything with him, I guess."

Cadigan could not speak, he could not even think. He closed his eyes in the darkness—his heart was aching and his head was swimming with bliss.

Then he could say, at last: "I'll come—to-morrow!"

"With Barney?"

"Yes, yes!"

Why did she have to insist so much on the dog?

"Well, I'm going to like you, I know," ventured Louise, grinning shamelessly behind the cover of the darkness as she sped this bolt at the heart of the man in the night.

Some emotions have electrc power, like the joy of Cadigan, which reached her with a thrill, though she could not see more than the dull outline of his form, where the two shadows were spilled awkwardly upon the ground.

"Do you know," said Cadigan, "that I think I could be happy around—this town of Gorman!"

She swallowed her laughter. After all, this fellow was too ridiculously simple!

"Louise!" broke in the thunder of Mr. Morris' voice. "Are you comin' instanter—young lady!"

There is nothing more dreadful than that title upon a father's tongue.

"Oh," said Lou, "I *do* have to go! Good-by—I don't even know your name!"

15

LOU MAKES A DISCOVERY

Her father caught her by the shoulder as she ran up to the back porch. Then he ushered her into the house at the end of his arm, giving her a little shake from time to time. She had never seen him in such a fury. They came into the dining room, which was the favorite sitting room of the family, also, and there young Rickie Morris looked up with a very broad grin of very malignant triumph. They were odd and sober rivals, that pair. However, his father's wrath descended even upon the head of Rickie.

"You grin, will you?" thundered Mr. Morris, his square-cut beard trembling with his wrath. "You grin, will you, you young hyena? Ain't you got no decency? Ain't you got no heart and no courage in you? Lettin' your sister perambulate around with every Tom, Dick, and Harry that comes into this here ornery town?"

"Dad," said the boy, grinding his teeth at these implied insults, "I guess you've said enough. I guess I don't have my duty pointed out twice!"

He leaped to the wall and snatched a revolver from a cartridge belt which hung there. Then he would have charged through the door had not the roar of his father stopped him again.

"Hey! Rickie! You young fool! Stand still, there! You want to throw yourself away, eh? You think that you'd look mighty pretty all dressed up in grave clothes, maybe, and planted around with flowers? Well, I don't aim to think so. I want to get *some* use out of you!"

"D'you aim to think that I'm afraid of that gent, just because he can do little tricks with dogs? Dad, I'm a little bit more of a man than that!"

A smiling sneer appeared upon the face of Mr. Morris. "I see," said he with a bitter grimace. "You know all about him, eh? You know just what manner of man he might be and what sort of a fighter he is, eh?"

"I dunno that I said all that," muttered the son, "but I ain't afeard of him. By the looks of his guns, besides, he ain't none too handy with guns. They was mighty old-fashioned. I had 'em in my hands!"

"Then," rumbled Morris, "you've had hold of a pair of guns that've killed more men than ary a pair of guns that ever come into the West!"

"Dad—is he a—a killer?"

"Them guns," rolled on the father, "they tell me belong to old man Uncle Joe Loftus!"

"Joe Loftus! Why—did this gent steal 'em from Uncle Joe, then?"

"Rickie, you got to learn not to interrupt. I was tellin' you that them guns by right belonged to Uncle Joe Loftus. But he *give* them to this here kid."

"He give away his guns?" muttered young Rickie, amazed. "Uncle Joe done that?"

"Maybe you want to know for why?"

"Sure I want to know for why!"

"Old Henks, he come over the mountains a week ago and he met up with Uncle Joe, and Loftus told him the same story. Seems like this here gent come up to Loftus to learn how to shoot. He stayed with him whole doggone months. And when he got through, doggone me if Loftus didn't give him the guns, because he was a better man than Loftus. That's a fact!"

"Loftus is mighty old."

"He's still poison, young man. Lemme tell you that. They don't breed no more Uncle Joes—no, not in these here times. They're too busy. They got quantity production, they have!"

[illegible]

things, don't you?"

"I don't aim to do all that," said Lou, shrugging her shoulders, for her father's tantrums imposed less upon her than upon the others. "All I know is that he talked mighty quiet and—and sort of nice, dad. Just like a boy!"

Her father threw up his hands in a gesture of the most terrible despair. "I've always knowed that Rickie was sort of stupid," said he. "But now you, too—Lou, he was just settin' by and makin' a fool out of you!"

Little Mrs. Morris, standing in a corner of the room, all this time had been growing more and more shaky. Now she dropped weakly into a chair and moaned: "Father, I can't stand it. Tell us what sort of a *devil* that man is!"

"Him?" said Mr. Morris, combing out the thick tangles of his short black beard with his fingers. "Him? I'll tell you about that *gentle* young man. Mrs. Morris, and you too, Rickie—and you, Lou, that knows so much; that young gent is the most dangerousest, most fightin'est gent in the whole mountains. And that's a fact. Danger ain't nothin' to him. Danger ain't nothin', I say. He lives by it. It's bread and meat to him, I guess. But I could sum it all up for you and tell you that his name is Cadigan!"

"Cadigan!" echoed Rickie, growing a little white and looking down at the gun which he still clasped in his right hand as he stood against the wall near the door.

"What's that?" asked Lou frankly.

"Don't you know *nothin'?*" groaned her father. "Don't you even know who Cadigan is?"

"I dunno that I do."

"Might you of heard of Bill Lancaster, Miss Morris?"

"Of course. Every one knows about Bill Lancaster being the best fighter in—"

"Everybody used to know. But everybody that's awake knows about Cadigan, now—because he's the gent that licked Bill Lancaster!"

It was truly a stunning blow to the girl. She had expected the wrath of her father, in spite of all of his lengthy preambles, to simmer down to nothing. She was used to such scenes, for Mr. Morris loved to make excitement, and use himself as the center of it.

But this was too much for the girl. She fled straightway to Sylvia Bender for confession and for sympathy. For Sylvia was her friend. Ever since her good advice had kept Sylvia from running away with the fake rancher who afterward turned out to be an escaped convict—ever since that thrilling night, Lou had been the bosom friend of Sylvia, and there was nothing between them except some slight jealousies which were bound to exist between the two prettiest girls in Gorman Pass. Now Lou carried all of her doubts to Sylvia and told her the whole story. After she had heard it Sylvia lowered her black eyes and frowned at a distant corner of the room.

"I dunno, Lou," she said at last. "It would seem all right—except that he talked so *awful* simple!"

"I know," said Lou wretchedly. "I keep thinkin' of that, too. I guess maybe all the time he was making a fool of me and laughing at me up his sleeve!"

"Oh, not as bad as all that!" said Sylvia, not too sympathetically. For, of late, the conquests of Lou had been a little too numerous for the equanimity of Sylvia Bender. "But I guess he was just stringin' you a little, Lou."

"I hate him!" said Lou fervidly.

"I guess you do," murmured Sylvia. "I'd hate a man that had strung me along like that."

"You don't have to forget Joe Riley—or Frankie—"

"Lou!"

"Oh, Sylvia, I'm sorry, but it makes me sick. I—I really liked him!"

"That's instinct, Lou. You had an instinct that told you there was something to him, after all!"

"Instinct your foot!" snapped out Lou with much spirit. "I'll tell you, he looked to me like a nice boy. And—I still [illegible]

[illegible] started a fight. Cadigan tied him in a knot and threw him into the hall. That's a fact, because my own father was in the hotel and saw it all."

It reduced Lou to utter silence.

"I guess I am a fool," she said at last. "I didn't guess he was that sort. But—"

"Well, Lou?"

"D'you think that he'll come for me tomorrow? D'you think that he'll come to see me, the way he promised?"

"Lou!" cried her companion. "Are you buildin' on that?"

But the head of Lou fell and she remained for a long time staring hopelessly at the floor.

"I wish you could of heard him talk," she said at last. "He was like a child—almost."

"I know, dear," said Sylvia. "I guess I've heard what kind of lies men can tell. Oh, Lou, they're terrible bad. I guess there ain' nothing in the world quite so bad as what a man can be. That Frank Wilson—I used to believe every word he said—like it was said in church, Lou!"

But here Lou arose and went to the door of the house.

"You won't do nothin' rash, Lou?"

"I hope he never comes near me again," exclaimed Lou. "The clever, worthless rascal!"

"That's just what he is, honey. I'm mighty glad that you begin to see through him."

"Oh," cried Lou, "what good does it do to see through 'em, Sylvia, except to make you more interested in 'em all!"

16

LANCASTER PLANS TROUBLE

It was at about this time that Duds Malone returned to the hotel, a sober and a solemn man. He went up the stairs and straight to the room where he found Bill Lancaster playing cribbage with Ches Morgan, while Sam Boswick lounged on a bed in the corner of the room, pretending to read a magazine, but now and again revealing the absent state of his gloomy mind by rolling his eye up and fixing it for a long time on nothingness. Duds Malone, for his part, dragged up a chair to the stove, opened the drafts, stoked it with more wood, and soon had the stove roaring like a high wind, while little red spots began to show through the thin metal.

"Hey!" exclaimed Ches Morgan. "This ain't a oven. We ain't bakin' bread, Duds."

"You go to the devil," said Duds fervently. "I'm cold. I got all chilled."

"Doin' what?" asked Ches sarcastically. "Huntin' our friend Cadigan?"

Bill Lancaster said nothing at all, but he glanced sharply

down and waited, pale with hope. Perhaps Cadigan had been brushed from his path!

"Maybe I have," said Duds Malone. "Maybe I've [illegible]

[illegible] prised at the temerity of his companion.

Duds snarled like a fighting terrier. "You ham head!" he shrilled at Sam. "You pork barrel! You thick-headed, slaw-jawed, cock-eyed rat. You double-jointed mud eater. Why darn your heart, d'you dare to talk back to a—man!"

His wild fury broke out like a volcano. In another instant there must have been gun play, and in such a mood it was a question whether Duds' fury would not have made him erratic enough to compensate for the greater slowness of Sam Boswick with a weapon. But here Bill Lancaster interrupted harshly. His own ire had been rising for some time, and as he saw his hopes for the destruction of Cadigan by another hand grow dimmer and smaller in the distance, he lost his temper all the more in proportion.

"All right," said Lancaster. "I guess that you've both had a chance to yap now. But I guess you'll listen to me for a spell. If either of you puts so much as the end of a finger nail on his gun, I'll blow the devil out of the both of you. And that's a fact and that's final. Understand? That's a fact and that's final!"

They glared at him in turn, but there was something so grim in the anger-blackened face of their captain that they changed their minds about action. It was no use to run into a wall of stone. So they abated their voices.

"What's happened to you?" went on Lancaster, as he saw that the crisis had passed. "What's happened to you, Duds? You went out aimin' to blow a hole through Cadigan. Seems like you've changed your mind, partner. Maybe you didn't like the looks of Cadigan so well when you got up close to him?"

But Malone had a tongue of his own, and he knew how to use it.

"After I figgered it all out," he said, "I seen that it wasn't hardly fair to you, Bill. Everybody knows that you been huntin' this Cadigan. And now it looks like Cadigan had been huntin' you. Seems from what I heard tell, later on, that he's been gettin' himself ready for the fun. He's been goin' to school like a good little boy."

"What kind of talk is this here, Duds?"

"He's been workin' out with old Uncle Joe Loftus and learnin' the old man's tricks."

Lancaster pushed his chair back from the table and raised his head.

"You never thought of doin' nothin' like that, did you?" asked the malicious Duds. "It might of polished up your style a mite, chief."

"That thick-headed young fool!" said Lancaster bitterly. "What could Loftus teach him? Loftus is a doddering old jackass."

"Sure, maybe he is," said Duds. "But before he got through teachin' this here Cadigan, he thought enough of him to give him his own guns to carry along!"

And now Lancaster, to cover the pallor which had swept across his face, rose suddenly and left the room. One step outside the door he paused to consider what he must do—or what he could do, for his heart was thundering in him and his spirit was fast failing. He strove to calm himself, to think.

So, as he stood there, he heard Duds Malone tell the story of how Cadigan had conquered Barney and how the town had stood by and wondered. That tale lost nothing by the telling which Malone gave it, and when he ended: "They's something doggone queer about Cadigan—he ain't like other men!" Mr. Lancaster agreed with him with all his heart.

Plainly he must meet Cadigan and meet him soon. Boswick had tried and been crushed. The nerve of Malone had failed him at the crucial moment. There remained only himself, and the world expected him to fight. Fight he must, or be shamed.

He went down to the veranda of the hotel and met the [illegible]

[illegible] out lookin' for trouble. That's all."

The sheriff smiled. "Maybe that's so," he said. "You aim to hunt him, or wait for him?"

"I never hunt trouble," said Lancaster quietly.

The sheriff grinned again in the dark. It was not hard for him to guess that this was not a quarrel exactly to the taste of the big gun fighter, in spite of all he had heard of the long trail Lancaster had ridden in pursuit of the younger man. In the meantime, Lancaster hastened to change the subject to another in which he was almost equally interested.

"How's things turning up about the P. & S. O. Railroad robbery, sheriff?" he asked. "I got nothin' to do just now. If you might need me on the trail, I could loan you a few days of my time."

"Thanks," said the sheriff heartily. "I appreciate that, Bill."

But there was a little reserve in his voice which Lancaster appreciated, and he went on to explain: "Mostly I don't take no interest in what happens," he said, "but when they begin to stick up trains—why, that's time to put a stop to things. Stickin' up a gent on the road, or even dragging out the till of a store—that ain't so bad, I guess. But a train robbery—that's pretty rank, Andrews!"

"It is," said the sheriff, smiting his fat hands together. "It's worse than bad! And I'll have the skunks before long. Between you and me, Lancaster, I know that they can't keep under cover very long, and the first gent that I hear of spreadin' hundred-dollar bills around loose and easy—I'll nab him! That was how they got most of the loot!"

Lancaster searched through his mind. But he could not recall that he or any of his party had as yet spent any of the hundred-dollar bills. A thick little sheaf of them at that moment was stowed inside the breast pocket of his coat. And the mind of Lancaster began to act rapidly. When a friend stepped up to the sheriff a moment later, Lancaster slipped away and up the stairs to the room of Cadigan. All was silent inside and no light showed in the crack beneath the door, so he pushed it open and entered. He could think of no better place. So he selected with care, groaning at the amount he was forced to give up, and put seven bills under the pillow on the bed. Seven hundred dollars was a great deal to spend, but an instinct told him that if he could send Cadigan to prison for that moment, it would be the cheapest investment of his life.

Then he tiptoed out through the listening darkness again and hastened down the stairs in time to rejoin the sheriff before that conversation had ended, and when the other departed, Lancaster took his place with the sheriff. Luckily the latter was still full of the robbery.

"About that train robbery," he said at once. "I've got a clew that leads clean away to Iowa, Lancaster, but the way I figger it—the boys that done that work belong right around these parts."

"How d'you figger that, sheriff?"

"By the way they scattered right after they done the work and then faded out. Each one of 'em had a map of these here mountains planted in his head. After the work was done, each of 'em knew just where to go to be safe. I figger that they've stayed scattered and are waitin' for the excitement to quiet down some."

"Ay," said Lancaster, breathing more easily, "it'd take a sort of a nervy gent to dare to show up right after an outrage like that holdup."

"It would," agreed the sheriff most emphatically.

"Still—" said Lancaster, in a heavy voice.

"Still what?"

"It's turnin' on cold like winter was pretty near here,

sheriff. When them stars get a frosty look, like they got now, it's time to think of findin' a warm place for the winter, I'd say."

The sheriff grunted. "Darn the winter," said he. "Be- [illegible]

[illegible]

pected ain't a friend of mine. Matter of fact, he's an enemy. People might think that I'd pointed him out so's I wouldn't have to fight him."

"By the eternal!" cried the sheriff. "You're speaking of Cadigan!"

"Are they saying that already?" asked Lancaster hotly. "Are they saying already that I ain't got the nerve to front up to that Cadigan?"

"Never mind what they say. Do you mean that you have some sort of a proof agin' Cadigan?"

"I ain't sayin' another thing. I ain't accusin' Cadigan. The way I'll accuse him will be with what my gat can say to him. Y'understand?"

"Sure. But the holdup—Lancaster, you got to talk! I can't arrest Cadigan without some sort of proof agin' him."

"I can't say nothin', sheriff. My tongue's tied by a promise. Besides, maybe they ain't nothin' in it. Maybe I'd be bringin' an innocent man into trouble. I wouldn't do that, Jeff, not even for you. You're a man I've always cottoned to, Andrews. I like the way you think and the way you're made inside and out. But I wouldn't hurt an innocent man, not even for you!"

This gentle speech was received by the sheriff with a muffled snort. "Well," he said, "I can't *make* you talk if you won't. But it's darned hard of you not to open up, I'll tell a man!"

"I'm doin' all for the best, sheriff."

"A darned queer way of thinkin' of the best, Lancaster. Tell me straight, what good is it gunna do me to have a suspicion of Cadigan with nothin' to work on?"

Lancaster, apparently, exploded with impatience. "I dunno," said he. "I ain't a mind reader, am I? I ain't able to see what *you* had ought to do. But what I know is that if I was in your boots I'd start makin' an investigation. I'd arrest this here Cadigan and search him, and I'd arrest him quick, because if you don't, I'll be finishing him with my gun, sheriff. I've heard a mighty lot of talk goin' on about be bein' afraid to tackle this Cadigan, and now I'm gunna show them how I work. They forget me and what I've done, that's what they do! But if I was you, I'd arrest Cadigan mighty pronto and then search him and maybe his whole room, too. If he's one of the crooks, he's apt to have some of his loot right along with him. Ain't that logical?"

"Sure," muttered the sheriff. "Or, why not start right in with the room—while Cadigan's out? Maybe I could get something on him that way and then surprise him. They ain't nothin' like a surprise, partner. Not a thing! Always got a good chance to scare a confession out of a crook if they think that you know it, anyway! But Cadigan—that soft-lookin' kid! Who'd of thought it!"

17

BARNEY VISITS A HOTEL

It was midnight before Cadigan stirred in the yard of the Morris home, and though he had not eaten since noon of that day, he felt no hunger. And if he were cold, he was insensible of it, and if he were weary he did not know it. For he was filled in every part of his being with an intense happiness, and most perfect satisfaction. For the first time in his life he had added to himself another being. Here was one who would come when he called, and stay when he bade it stay.

Now, when he rose to his feet, Barney rose with him. The rope was not needed to guide him. When Cadigan walked from the yard, Barney strode beside him, his gigantic head near the hip of his master. Still, Cadigan kept a tight grip on the leash. How could he tell what would happen if another man came close to the killer.

He hurried straight down the street to the hotel. He had waited purposely until it was late so that there would be no one in the lobby when he entered, and he was right. An oil lamp was turned low on the central table, but there was no one in sight. Visitors did not arrive in Gorman at midnight. At the door, Barney paused with a deep, murmuring growl, but when Cadigan walked on, with a slight twitch at the rope, Barney looked up into the face of the man and wagged his tail slightly.

He did not like it at all. In his long forest career the wild dog had learned that there were few things which he needed to fear. If he crossed the trail of a bobcat, no matter how big, he did not have to give way with his tail between his legs, for what could hold off a whole pack of domesticated dogs could be destroyed with one crunch of the jaws of Barney. Even if he came on the sign of a mighty lofer wolf, he could follow that trail if he chose. He could travel until he sighted them, and when the wolf was sighted, Barney could run the beast down! And when he had run it down, he could kill it offhand. Against wolfish cunning he could pit an equally cruel and equally tricky skill combined with something more—the brain of a dog! More adroit, fleeter, stronger, he had hunted them for pleasure and killed them many a time; the scars of their teeth were hidden by his bushy fur. He could kill the lofer wolf, therefore, and everything beneath the dignity of the lofer. Or again, he could trail a bull moose through the northern forests when the snow hampered its activity, and he could circle around it until he saw his opening and leap in to hamstring the monster.

Such was the range of his destructive powers, but there were limits even for Barney. Mr. Grizzly, for instance, was distinctly bad medicine, and though he might be followed and studied from the distance, it was exceedingly wise never to come to grips with that clever giant. There was the mountain lion, too, a cowardly but terrible fighter, which could rip out the belly of Barney with a single stroke of its knifelike claws. Once, long and long before, Barney had fallen foul of a young lion. He had killed the creature, but for a month thereafter his wounds had nearly put an end to him. And that was one of the cardinal lessons of his rough life. But though the grizzly was terrible and the mountain lion hardly less so, there was another danger greater than either—greater than both combined.

It came from a slow-moving creature with no great power of eye, with a ridiculous dullness of ear which amounted almost to deafness, and certainly with no nose whatever—a futile, easily tired, blundering thing which sometimes perished of cold in the mid-wnter, and which sometimes was destroyed by the heat of the desert even if [illegible]

valley beneath him.

That was his first view of man, but he never forgot. Afterwards, he saw mountain lions and bears die by the sightless weapon of man, while the voice of the gun spoke heavily a little later. Besides, man had other powers. It gave cruel life to wood and steel and made it lie in wait, ready to grip the unwary passer-by. It filled the woods with the terror of its brains.

So, during his capitivity, schooled by the club and the harsh voice of young Rickie Morris, the fear and the hate of Barney had grown. Now that Cadigan had come to him, he made no mistake. It was not the same. Cadigan was different. Just as he, Barney, was different from other dogs, such as he had seen wolves kill with ease, such as he himself had killed with a single stroke when the packs hunted him ever and anon. Just as Barney was like a dog and yet different, so was Cadigan like other men, and yet different. His hand was strong, yet his touch gentle. His voice was deep, but it fell softer on the ear than the sound of running water.

And here was this man taking him, Barney, into a den filled with an inextricable tangle of the scents of other men, unknown men, who had tainted the pure air of the mountains with the foul odors of tobacco, leather boots—and guns! There were always guns. Cadigan himself carried them, though no doubt they were different from other guns just as their master was different from other men. Still, Cadigan went straight ahead. How carelessly he crossed a hundred trails, any one of which could have given an hour's employment to the studious nose of Barney!

Now, behold, he was advancing into the upper regions of this cave. He went up a great hollow log, niched for greater ease in climbing, and proceeding calmly into the upper darkness. Oh, how rash and yet how wonderful were the ways of men!

At the head of the stairs, Cadigan made no pause. Neither to the right nor to the left did he look, while Barney, shuddering with dread, slunk behind him, hoping that all would turn out well, but possessed with mighty doubts. For who could tell, when danger was everywhere, from what direction it would strike, and who would be its victim?

Once, when a man snored in an adjoining room, he dropped flat to the floor and waited, tense, for the attack. But the soft voice of the master reassured him, and Barney rose and permitted himself to be persuaded down the hall.

They paused before a door which was presently opened. And Cadigan stepped in. But Barney paused on the threshold, frozen with dread and with hatred. For the air was thick with the scent of man—not of one, but of many. The window was open, with a steady breeze blowing through which sifted the odors and carried them to him in distinct streams. Yonder was one scent coming from the corner, and another from behind the bed, and another issued from behind a partially closed door. There were more, so many that confusion seized upon Barney. Worse than all, every man scent, among them all, came to him commingled with the terrible odor of guns, the biting sharp odor of powder, which is the sign of the winged death!

So Barney crouched, bracing himself, his mane bristling.

"Steady boy!" said Cadigan. "What's wrong with you? Here's where we bunk down."

He took another step into the darkness, but as he did so, nature rebelled in Barney. He would have fled, except that he could not, somehow, leave the man behind him in such surroundings. A growl burst from his throat—rather a roar of rage and terror than a growl, and at the sound there were half a dozen half-stifled exclamations from within the room.

Here, at last, the master was alarmed. He leaped straight back through the doorway with two guns whip- [illegible]

had been empty when they came there, now appeared two shadowy figures, tall men with the dull glimmer of guns in their hands. And, though it was dark, enough illumination came through a hall window to show them to Cadigan and to show Cadigan to them.

With all his soul Barney dreaded confronting them, but he had no choice. He was the cornered rat; beyond them, lay liberty. He flung himself at them ready to die, but to kill if he could. His shoulder struck one and knocked him sprawling against the wall. His teeth, aimed at the throat of the second man, missed as the fellow twitched away from this flying apparition which had risen from the floor—the teeth of Barney missed the throat, but they struck the shoulder instead. Through the coat those glistening fangs ripped as through rotten cheesecloth, and like knives—dull, tearing knives—they plunged into the flesh of the arm. There was a wild yell of agony and of fear; then, through the opened way, fled Barney with the man behind him.

After them raged the torrent of the pursuit. But the darkness which had helped to set the trap for Cadigan was now a help to bring him back to liberty. The first rush of the sheriff's men clogged the doorway of the room in which Cadigan had expected to sleep. Then, as they stumbled into the hallway, they saw the man at the heels of the beast whip around the corner of the corridor and make for the stairs.

They followed as fast as they could. Half of them

sprawled over the two prostrate figures on the floor of the hall. The others with their guns poised leaped for the head of the stairs. One man got a flying shot at man and beast as they hurtled through the front doorway of the hotel into the outer dark. And that was their last glimpse of Cadigan.

It might not have been their last. It was discovered afterward, to the incredible dismay of the town, that Cadigan had actually dared to pause in his flight to saddle his own mustang, mount it, and ride calmly away with the great wolf dog before him.

But the men of the sheriff's party were busy for a fatal minute delaying their pursuit in order to say to one another: "How did he get away?"

18

NEWS AT THE FARMHOUSE

All through the night Cadigan fled with the horror behind him. What had happened he could not tell except, very certainly, that law-abiding men had united to cast him forth, and they had cast him forth at the very time when he had at last found a woman. *The* woman, she was, in the mind of Cadigan. He thought of the world as a place filled with many men, cunning, treacherous, savage, cruel, remorseless, dangerous—and one woman, a green island in the gray of ocean, a glimpse of heaven and happiness in the long winter of his life.

Yet as he rode along through the darkness, it could not be said that he was not happy. For he had left behind him the promise that he would return, and it was a sweet claim against him, and a hope for happiness again. So, as he rode, he forgot Barney, even; and forgot the very horse he rode on, passing through a sort of region of dreams until he came to the gray of the dawn and the cold realization of the truth.

He had come out through the mountains over no trail, driving along with only a northern star to guide him, and so he had reached, in the heart of the peaks, a little valley with a floor of gently rolling ground—a scant quarter section of rich pasture and even of ploughed land. There was a small farmhouse in the center of that little kingdom and Cadigan, weary, hungry, cold, knew that he would have to take shelter here and get food before he went on. Neither he nor his horse were fit for much longer stretch without some renewing of their vigor.

He hesitated for only a moment. It could not be, he felt, that news of the night before had come this way. Whatever they thought he had done as a crime—and God knew that he had no knowledge of a crime in his mind—the word of it could not have come to this isolated house. Moreover, the curling of smoke from the chimney, at that moment, came to Cadigan like a word of peace and good will in the midst of the wilderness. As he started, Barney ranged before him through the gray of the morning, and Cadigan saw him and thought of him for the first time in hours. He saw him, too, with a start and with a shudder. He was like that, now, from henceforward, perhaps—an outlaw in the world—neither dog nor wolf!

When he dismounted and tapped, a woman in a gingham wrapper came to the back door and peered out at him with a frown which was not of fear.

"Be you a tramp, young man?" she asked.

"Ma'am," said Cadigan, "I started out from Gorman last night, but I got lost, and I've rode all this time without knowin' just where I was about to wind up. I tried to get back to town, but I found out that I'd lost my way."

"You ain't lost it bad," said she. "Gorman ain't more'n a step across the hills."

"No?" echoed Cadigan, starting at such unwelcome news.

"About five miles," said the woman.

Her eyes ran over his figure to his boots and rested carefully upon them. They were soundly made and of good quality. This decided her that she had to do with no vagabond.

"Put up your hoss and give him a snack of something, will you?" she said. "Hey, Tom, come out and take care of this boy and his hoss, will you?"

But Cadigan excused himself carefully and went out to the stable by himself; he had no wish that the farmer should issue forth and find the wolf dog waiting. But Barney had disappeared. Perhaps he had gone forever. [illegible] chatting with the wife. She told him of the barley crop, while she mxed sour-milk biscuits, rolled them out, cut them from the sheet of dough, and laid them in a greased pan, and slammed the door of the oven upon the pan. She told him of the barley crop and of herself and her husband. Tom, who came to lean in the doorway, at last, a tall, weary, thin man, whose Adam's apple bobbled up and down in his throat as he talked. They lived here alone, raising a few cattle, a little barley and wheat, economizing closely, dreading the terrible winter of the mountains.

They had breakfast on the kitchen table, because it was the only warm room in the house, and as they sat down, the blow fell.

"What time did you leave Gorman?" asked the farmer.

"Along in the evenin'," said Cadigan noncommittally.

"Maybe you didn't hear about this gent Cadigan, then?"

Cadigan's blood chilled. "What about him? I've heard his name."

"Sure. We've all heard that. Everybody knows how he stood up to Lancaster and how Lancaster is after him now. Well, it turns out he's a real bad un. It's him that done the P. & S. O. holdup!"

Cadigan started. That was it, then. It was this crime which they had laid upon him.

"He did that?" said he.

"He sure did. They found some of the money in his room, under his pillow. A fool place to keep as much as seven hundred dollars, I'd tell a man! Half a dozen boys from Gorman rode through here after midnight and dropped in for a bite and a cup of coffee. They told us. Besides, this here Cadigan, seems that he got hold of that cattle-killin' devil—that wolf—or dog that acts like a wolf—Barney. He got hold of that dog, Barney, and tamed it in a couple of hours. Don't seem nacheral, does it?"

"It don't," agreed Cadigan, breathing hard.

He was treated to a detailed account of some of the exploits of Barney. When the ham and eggs were finished, they passed back to the subject of himself.

"The boys from Gorman are hot after him," said Tom. "The railroad is offerin' a mighty fat reward for the arrest of them robbers."

"What sort of a lookin' man is he?" asked Cadigan. "I don't hanker to meet up with his likes."

"About your age and size, they told me," said Tom. "Gimme some more of that coffee, Martha."

Martha had reached for the coffee pot when she dropped her hand suddenly and, looking at the window at the side of the room, screamed loudly. Cadigan turned his head in time to see the shadowy form and the great, wicked head of Barney disappearing. He had reared up, perhaps, to look in at the master.

There was no opportunity to evade the issue. The truth seemed to strike home in man and wife at the same instant. The farmer leaped to his feet and stood transfixed; poor Martha cowered in her chair; and both stared with terrible fear at Cadigan. All the blood in his body rushed to his head, then receded and left him wonderfully cool.

Tall Tom had gripped a rifle which leaned against the wall, and Cadigan now slipped out one of Uncle Joe's revolvers. The woman moaned at the sight of it.

"I'd ride along and bother you no more," said Cadigan gravely to them, "but I got to have a rest. I got to sleep, and my hoss has got to rest and eat. Y'understand? So I'm gunna stay right here. You can show me to a bedroom, Tom."

They both herded before him and his gun through the narrow, damp hallway, and into a little bedroom where the clothes were still in disorder.

"Now," said Cadigan, "you can run along and do your

chores, ma'am. But your husband'll stay here with me. I'm gunna set him down in that chair and tie him into it. If he tries to get loose—I'll wake up and finish him. You see?"

[illegible]

house. He locked the door; the farmer submitted without a word, merely staring with great eyes of horror while Cadigan made him fast to the chair; then Cadigan rolled himself in the bedding and was instantly asleep.

He wakened at the end of a full eight hours only when the sun of the mid-afternoon began to stream through the window. Then he sat up and yawned. That sleep had renewed his strength threefold. A glance at his watch told him the time; and there was Tom, slipped far down in his chair, sound asleep. He started like a frightened child when Cadigan loosened him from the bonds. Then they went out into the kitchen together and Cadigan would never forget the haunted face of the poor wife or the "Thank God!" which she breathed at the sight of her husband in the flesh in spite of all her fears.

"D'you think," asked Cadigan, "that I'd kill for the sake of killin'?"

"I don't think nothin'," said the farmer. "You've got me, Cadigan. I ain't no fightin' man. I ain't got no money you can take. But I got supplies, and you can help yourself in the kitchen."

"I'll do without robbin' you," said Cadigan, and he even found it possible to smile. "Stay right inside the house, Tom, till I'm out of sight. After that, you can start for Gorman as fast as you want, to tell 'em the news."

With this he went out to the stable, and when he had saddled his horse and led it forth into the sun, Barney appeared around the edge of the barn. The line of his belly was no longer gaunt, and on the white of his silken broad vest there was a dark dappling of blood. Plainly the brute had killed and eaten and slept well after his kill!

So they passed across the farm lands and went on straight north, away from Gorman, with Cadigan still puzzling out the manner in which he could have ridden in such a circle the night before. After he had crossed the second ridge of the hills, however, he turned again south, keeping himself on rocky ground where there would be slight chance of picking up the sign of his trail. He came back to the ridge of hills overlooking the town of Gorman. There he waited until the evening, and when the dusk had thickened over the woods, he started down for the house of Morris.

19

BENEATH LOU'S WINDOW

There was one great embarrassment, however. He could leave his horse tethered on the edge of the woods, but no rope would hold Barney. The strong teeth of the dog would have slashed through the stoutest hemp in no time. Therefore it only remained for Cadigan to take the monster with him—and at what a risk of discovery if he did so! One murderous growl from Barney might bring a dozen men looking for him with guns in their hands. He could only pray that the dog would fight, if a fight came, as the wolves do, silently!

But it was all easier than he had expected. He started down at a point exactly opposite to the house of Harrison Morris, and presently he was at the dining-room window looking in at the whole family assembled. He had come in the nick of time, it seemed to Cadigan, to find himself the object of discussion. But as a matter of fact, had he come at any hour of that day, he would have found their tongues wagging on the same subject. Or in any house in all of Gorman, he would have found the same thing true.

The town had received a shock such as had never come to it before; and it could think of nothing else.

Harrison Morris began the talk, as was fitting from the head of the family. He was first seen buried behind a small mountain newspaper. Now he lowered it and pushed his spectacles up on his forehead.

"Well," he said, "it's all right in here. They even know your nickname, Rickie. Doggone me if the reporters ain't slick! Think of a town like Newsom havin' a paper like this! Slapped the news right out, too. Printed an extra, doggone me if they didn't!"

"Read it aloud, dad," pleaded young Richard.

The father adjusted the glasses and squinted down his nose.

"You read it, Lou," he said. "You got a way of rappin' out the words faster'n I could."

Lou took the paper, and her first word was an exclamation of protest.

Ruffian Terrorizes Gorman! she read, and cried: "That's not true!"

"If he didn't throw a scare into Gorman, you go and ask some of the boys ag'in'." said her brother shrewdly. "Doggoned if I ain't free to admit that he throwed a man-sized scare into *me!*"

"I don't mean that!" answered Lou. "Perhaps he terrorized Gorman; I mean that he isn't a ruffian!"

There was a shout from the rest of the family.

"He's got you buffaloed!" exclaimed her father.

"He's got a mighty lot softer voice than anybody in my family," protested the girl hotly. "I won't read any more of this silly paper. Besides, it isn't true!"

"What ain't true?"

"That he tore up the town and left two wounded men—"

"What *did* happen to 'em? How did they get a tore shoulder and a fractured skull?"

"Barney did it!"

"And who owns that dog?"

"I don't care," said Lou with a beautiful disregard of logic. "It's not true!"

"Look at the way she talks," said Rickie. "Doggone me if I ain't ashamed to hear you talk like that, Lou! This here Cadigan, he looks easy, but that's because he's a sight harder'n any man you ever see in your life. Crooked, that's what he is."

"You're right, boy," said Harrison Morris. "That's

[illegible]

they's an oldish gent named Morgan that'll be heard from. The boys are gunna turn out in four parties and start tomorrow mornin'. They'll go up to the farmhouse where he tried to murder the old man and woman today and pick up the trail there."

"That's the biggest lie yet!" exclaimed the girl. "I know he didn't try to do no murdering! He's too good-natured for that."

Cadigan, the blood thundering at his temples, blessed her faith with all his heart. Then she rose.

"I'm going to bed," she announced. "I'm tired of hearing what people think. I'd like to hear what they *know!*"

"You think this here Cadigan is pretty fine, eh?"

"I do!"

"He didn't rob no train, maybe?"

"What if he did?"

"Oh," sneered Rickie, "that don't amount to nothin', I guess."

"How do you know he robbed the train, anyway?"

"Wasn't the money found in his bed?"

"I don't care what he did," said the girl. "I can tell a man when I see one!" And she stormed through the door. There she turned and fired a parting shot.

"You'd be mighty proud of yourself if you'd done half what Cadigan has done, Rickie—you big—hulk!"

Rickie rose, stuttering with fury. "Him? That crook?" he cried. "I—I—I'll go out and get that Cadigan myself!" yelled Rickie to the closed door, for Louise had already gone, slamming the door behind her. "I'll go get him and I'll collect that there reward, and I'll bring back the skin of that wolf dog myself!"

"Set down, Rickie," advised the mother gently. "Don't go rilin' yourself up over what Lou says. She don't mean nothin' by it. Not a thing, Rickie!"

So much Cadigan waited to hear, then, as a light glimmered through a window toward the front of the house, he hastened toward it; so that when Louise Morris raised the window, she found herself looking down into the darkness at two shadows in the night—one a man and one the unmistakable mighty outlines of Barney. He heard her draw in her breath with a gasp.

Then she dropped to her knees, which brought her face hardly a foot above his own.

"Cadigan! Cadigan! Are you a crazy man?" she cried softly to him.

"I gave you a promise," said he. "I come down to do what I'd said that I'd do. I come back to see you today, you know. I said I'd come."

"Hush!" whispered the girl. "They're all around—waiting for you. They're—they're just crazy to get you, Cadigan. Do you know about the rewards?"

"I've heard a little. The railroad is—"

"Everybody has joined in. All the rich ranchers and lumbermen and miners—every one puts in a few hundred to make that reward bigger. It's a fortune—mighty near. They'll never stop hunting till they get you, unless you go away, out of the country. Over the sea, Cadigan!"

He said nothing.

"But did you do it?" she asked eagerly.

"No! I never held up a train in my life, nor ever helped to hold up a train. I stuck up an old farmer for chuck and a sleep today. That's the first thing that I ever stole. But they drove me to that."

"You didn't try to kill the poor old man? Not really?"

"Does he say that?"

"That you—you shot at him as you were leaving, and that the bullet just missed his head."

"Some gents is born liars and some get that way by practice," said Cadigan. "I guess he's both. What would I of gained by killin' him?"

"That's what I told them all. But they laughed at me. They think that they know." She added: "What'll you do?"

[illegible]

forgive myself, Cadigan! But I could help you—I could get you supplies—and then—" She stopped, and one of those deadly silences fell between them.

"What can I do for you tonight?" she asked at last. "Poor fellow; there aren't many to stand by you now!"

"It's Lancaster," said Cadigan, his voice turning iron, "He's the one that's behind everything. It's Lancaster that has done me wrong. But him and me is due to meet up, some day!"

"What do you need, Cadigan?"

"Nothin'. Except, maybe—could you turn your head a mite so's the light would fall on your face?"

She could not help but obey, with the blood hot in her face and a pulse beating in her lips. And Cadigan came closer under the window. There he stood while the wind out of the trees played against her, and the odor of the wet woods poured into her room. It seemed to impress Lou Morris, at that moment, that the man before her represented all the great outdoors, rough and simple, and strong and true.

"All you could do for me would be to let me come again," said Cadigan. "Let me come tomorrow night."

"They'll catch you, Cadigan."

"Not while you want me to come," said he. "And the next time, besides, I'll have something to say. I'll think things up. I'll turn some of the things that are inside me into words. But all of today I've just been waitin' for the chance to see you. You understand?"

Barney stirred with a low-pitched growl, then reared up and planted his forepaws against the wall of the house —a mighty figure with his head as high as the head of the man!

"He's a mite jealous," said Cadigan, and passed his arm over the heavily muscled shoulders of the brute.

"He loves you," said the girl. "Hush!"

Voices passed down the street and paused before the house.

"You must go!" she whispered.

"May I come again?"

"No, no! Yes—if you wish to."

"Tomorrow night?"

"Not so soon. They'll make this a trap for you—yes, if you wish to come, Cadigan."

"Yes," said he. "I wish to come."

"Good night!"

"Good night."

She watched him draw back, still with his face turned toward her, until the darkness thickened around him, and his figure was lost to her.

Then she hurried to the mirror and found a flushed, startled face looking back to her, the eyes wide with excitement and something like fear.

"He loves me!" said Lou to herself, and then laughed silently at the image in the glass. "He loves me! Poor thing!"

Just why she pitied him for that she herself could not have told. But when she was undressing she began to sing, softly, so that the sound could not escape from her room.

Afterward she lay awake for a long time, and when she fell asleep, it was to dream of Cadigan breaking through a host and beating off a hundred dangers—all to come beneath her window in the night.

20

ANOTHER CRIME CHARGED TO CADIGAN

Sam Boswick, that same night, parted with his fellows. They had their last argument over the division of the spoils and a hot debate it was, with the three ranged steadfastly upon one side and Boswick resolute upon the other.

It was the weight of Lancaster which turned the scales against him.

"We all take our chances," said Lancaster. "You took an extra lot of work this time; the next time some other one of us'll do an extra share. That's fair and square all around. They ain't no use tryin' to make a pig out of yourself, Boswick!"

Boswick swelled with malice. "You're sore," he said, "because you planted some of your coin on poor Cadigan to make him the goat!"

Lancaster struck his fist on the table. "Why, you fool," said he, "ain't that takin' the danger off of all our heads?"

"It is," broke in Ches Morgan earnestly. "That was a mighty smart turn, I'd say."

"You've give up part of your shares," said Boswick,

"and now you want to stick me. You want to beat me out of my rights. Well, Lancaster, I'm done with the lot of you. I'd as soon paddle my own canoe after this. Gents, so long."

So he rolled his blankets and left them without another word, but telling himself savagely that if God were willing he would find a way to repay them for their injustice. For such it seemed to him in an honest conviction. And, since honest convictions were luxuries in the mind and in the life of Mr. Samuel Boswick, he clung to this handy one with all his heart.

It made his face black and his heart still blacker as he spurred out of Gorman on this night. And, as he rode, he drove the spurs deep and damned the road, rutted since the recent rains. Then he cursed the wind which flapped the brim of his sombrero down over his eyes, and the rushing clouds which sailed across the heavens and made the moon small and dull behind them.

So he went hurtling down Gorman Pass until the stench of his sweating horse was thick in his nostrils and the poor beast grunted and labored in its stride. Three miles south and east of the town he swung aside onto the road which led toward Newsom. In Newsom he intended to find a bed that night, and then go on, he knew not where, but somewhere that promised action and money, and a chance, in the end, to sharpen a knife which Lancaster and the others would feel.

He climbed to the top of the southern ridge of hills which framed Gorman Pass, and as he did so, the rumble of wheels crossing a bridge in the heart of the next valley before him reached his ears, and then the voice of the driver, blown to him clear in the wind, but small with distance; last of all, he even heard the chucking of the hubs against the axles as a heavy load was tugged up the slope. It was the stage from Newsom coming to Gorman, and coming late, hence the hurry of the driver who was trotting up a slope along which he ordinarily would have walked his horses.

The mind of big Sam Boswick was made up on the spur of the moment. For immediate cash he had no need. His share of the plunder, even though it were only half of what he thought was due to him, was a larger sum than he had ever crowded into his wallet before in all his life. It was not a matter of money, but it was the malice against the entire world and the "injustice of men" which determined him. He wanted action and wanted it badly— [illegible] it by merely tugging down the brim of his hat. In this manner he converted his face to a white blur surmounted by a thick shadow out of which there was only visible the glimmer of his eyes. It left nothing about him that was recognizable. His down-headed horse was a tough mustang, not very fast, but as durable as steel; it was ugly enough to have passed for the horse of any man. His apparel was exactly what ninety-nine out of every hundred men in the mountains would be wearing. And now, having made sure of himself, he received a touch of grace from the elements, for the wind, which had been blowing from the south, swung sharply around into the east, and in a trice had scattered away the clouds which lay before the face of the moon. There was revealed a great, thick, silver disk floating in the blueblack of the sky, and showering down thin light over the mountains and over the massed trees of the forest.

All was well with Sam Boswick. He took this as a sign of luck and a proof that his adventure could not fail. So he drew his revolver, tightened his reins, freshened the grip of his knees, and waited while the voice of the driver damned the horses up the hill.

The leaders swung into view, bringing the rattle of the coach loudly behind them as they turned the bend of the road. Behind them labored the pointers with their heads down, working their best, and last of all the heavy wheelers with the tall coach rocking and jolting behind.

One touch of the reins brought Boswick to the heads of

the leaders. They stopped with a snort, while the driver whirled his long-lashed whip over his head and cursed the intruder for a fool. But the lash never fell. The gun tipped up in the hand of Sam Boswick, and he fired—perilously close to the head of the driver—so very close, indeed, that it blew the hat off his head.

"Now," said the amiable robber, "I'll knock off your head after your hat, if you don't mind what I say and stop the squealing of that fool in the coach!"

This last referred to the noisy lamenting of a girl in the coach who had heard the shot and looked out in time to see the brigand, mask and gun and all, in the bright moonshine.

"Shut her up," said Boswick, enjoying himself immensely, "or I'll cut her throat for her. Darned if I don't hate a yappin' fool of a woman!"

"For heaven's sake, ma'am," said the stage driver, "you'll get us all murdered. Stop that bawling!"

This was not distinctly chivalrous. But in fact, that was not exactly a chivalrous stage driver. He had worked a whip behind teams of six horses for thirty years. He had developed rheumatism and an amazing vocabulary during that space of years, but he had not lost his love of his life, and since this was the ninth or tenth time that he had been stuck up on the high road, he took it all very largely as a matter of course, like a philosopher.

The bawling stopped. Perhaps the lady was more shocked than frightened. At any rate, the tears which now ran down her cheeks were rather of rage than of terror.

"I never heard such language used!" cried she.

"You'll hear worse, though," said the stern Boswick, "if I got to talk to you any more about your noise. Pile down off'n that seat, driver. Pronto, too. I'm hurried, and my temper ain't good tonight. I'm late for supper already."

The driver climbed down to the ground, holding one hand well above his head and steadying himself with the other.

"Right-hand vest pocket," he said sourly to Boswick. "They's three one-dollar bills there. They's an old pocket knife with one blade in my right hip pocket, if you want that, and a slug of Star chewin' terbaccy in the left hip pocket, about half gone, and that's about all I got. Reach in and find out, if you don't believe me."

"You're a cool old oyster," said Boswick, grinning behind his mask in spite of himself. "Lemme see. old- [illegible] I ain't got you in the corner of my eye."

"Son," said the driver, "my holdup manners is perfect. I've had practice."

"The rest of you," barked Sam Boswick, "hop out of that there coach and do it quick. I ain't partial to no delays. Hop out and keep them hands up while you're hoppin'. You hear me?"

There were only four—the general merchandise store's proprietor, back from Newsom on a buying trip, two cow-punchers who were coming up into the mountains to forget the range and swing an ax in a lumber camp during the winter months, and last of all, the girl who had "squealed," as Boswick so inelegantly put it.

Boswick went first through the coach itself. In spite of their haste to get up their hands when they first sighted him, he found that the wallets of every one of them had been dropped to the floor of the coach and there they lay—a simple and an easy harvest for his hands.

He gathered them, pinching each one. Plainly their contents were of negligible importance—all except that of the proprietor. Boswick did not even give the others a glance, but tossed them back. With that single prize—a thick, squashy mass of bills inside the leather—he jumped back to the ground. Going through their pockets was a more profitable labor. He collected one gold watch and two good silver ones, besides a handful of silver, an excellent hunting knife from one of the punchers, and a bracelet from the girl.

At this robbery, as he slipped it rudely over her wrist, she protested loudly.

"It's my mother's only gift to me!" sobbed the girl. "It's all I got from her. It's a heirloom, Mr. Bandit. It cost her a year's savin's, she told me!"

The bandit swept his eye over the others. There was nothing to fear from them. The driver had set them a good example of submission, and they had followed it with the most scrupulous care. So Boswick centered his attention upon the lady. She was young. She was passably fair—at least she seemed so in the flattering light of the moon. And Boswick put his hand under her chin and raised her head.

She blinked at him in fear.

"Hon," said he, "tell me the straight of it. How much did that there bracelet cost you?"

"Twenty-three dollars and fifty cents, honest!" moaned the girl.

"Which your ma paid, or you?"

"I worked honest for every cent!"

"Well," said Boswick, brutally, "the thing is just plate. It ain't worth the fifty cents, let alone the twenty-three dollars. And here it is back."

He dropped it, as he spoke, down the inside of the neck of her dress. It was the sort of a joke that Mr. Boswick could appreciate. Then he leaned and kissed her liberally.

There was a squeal and a protesting flurry, but Boswick stepped back, laughing.

"I'll drop in and call on you, one of these nights," said he.

"Don't you dare!" cried the girl, fishing eagerly for the bracelet. "Who are you to—"

Boswick slipped onto the back of his horse again. "I'm Cadigan—that's all," he told them, and as their startled exclamations rang out about his ears, he backed his horse around the curve, then wheeled it and made off down the slope at full gallop.

But there was no pursuit. That name of Cadigan had paralyzed them, and the store proprietor voiced all their thoughts when he said: "We're mighty lucky to have our lives left us by that butcher!"

21

SYLVIA PLANS

Sylvia Bender brought the news to Louise Morris the next morning. She herself had heard the story with a good many minor decorations and she herself added a few more trimmings which had to do chiefly with what had happened between the bandit and Florence Curry, to whom he had restored the bracelet. And Louise listened with a shadow in her fine eyes.

"That's your man you thought so simple," said Sylvia in the end. "He's just a philanderer, dear. There are some like that. They pretend to be simple, but they're only playing a part. I *know!*"

Then, seeing that the face of Lou was downcast in thought, she added earnestly: "I guess you've not taken him too seriously, dear. Why, Lou, he's just plain no good!"

"Take him seriously?" said Lou, trying to laugh to keep the tears in her eyes from notice. "I—I despise him, Sylvia! I hate him!"

She broke off, turning her head away toward a sound of hounds opening in a pealing cry down the pass. She was glad to turn her head, moreover, from the searching eyes of her friend.

"What's that?" she asked.

"That's the Bill Symond pack," said Sylvia. "Lancaster sent for them. And Mr. Symond is coming with him. They're going to run Cadigan with the dogs, if they get a chance."

A picture formed in the mind of Lou of a solitary fugitive hurrying over a steep mountain trail on a spent horse with the noise of the pack rolling heavily behind him. She shivered at the thought, and yet it gave her a savage satisfaction.

"I hope they have the chance!" she cried angrily. "I hope they have the chance, and I hope they get him. Did he—did he really—kiss her?"

"Who? Florence Curry? Of course he did. They all saw it. They all say so. And he promised to come to see her. Can you imagine such a thing as that, Lou? Can you possibly imagine it?"

But Lou, setting her teeth, could imagine it very well. Had not just such a promise been made to her? It was a common bait scattered at large by the villain, it seemed!

The noise of the dogs came rapidly up the street and it was Lou's suggestion that brought them both to the front yard to see them pass. It was a veritable dog army which finally came into view—a full score of animals of every breed. Far to the rear, keeping discreetly just in front of the hoofs of Bill Symond's horse, came two bloodhounds, the brains of the pack when it came to a trail puzzle, of course. In front of them ranged the fighting force. They were cross-bred Airedales; there were great wolfish dogs, scarred and formidable; there were three or four short-haired mongrels which had earned a place in that army by often proved fighting ability. The whole swept by with a confused clamor.

"They've hunted mountain lions and lobos with that pack," said Sylvia in awe, and the dust cloud formed thick in the rear of the pack and its attendant riders.

"But will they hunt men?" asked the other girl.

"They've done it already."

"Where?"

"Bill Symonds comes from the South," said Sylvia, and did not need to finish her sentence.

"It's too horrible!" murmured Lou. "I thought—no, God help him if he ever comes in range of them. They'd

[illegible]

"Not a bit," said Sylvia with a sort of gloomy enthusiasm. "If you'd listened to some of my stories about 'em, you'd have known that! But, Lou, you're half crying. What in the world is the matter?"

"Sylvia," cried the girl, "they'll catch him tonight. There isn't a chance that they can fail to catch him! Because—"

"What in Heaven's name do *you* know about him, Lou?"

"He's coming here."

"Here?"

"To my house. He was here last night. He said that he was coming again."

"Let the dogs get him," cried Sylvia furiously. "Because, if the boys know this, they'll lynch him if they ever catch him! Lou, Lou, don't tell me that you've seen him and that you meant to see him again?"

"I couldn't help it. He was—like a child, Sylvia. If you'd seen him—"

"Lou, you actually care for him!"

"No—I—"

"I wish he were dead," said honest Sylvia. "He's managed to make you think that he's—oh, I could kill him for this!"

"He's not bad. I really can't think that he's bad!"

"And this about Florence Curry—"

"That silly little fool!" said Lou without charity. "I don't blame any man for treating her cheaply."

"But," began Sylvia. Then she changed her mind. If it

were necessary to argue, the case was already lost. For Sylvia was very wise in the ways of her own sex, even if she were not so wise in the ways of the rulers of the world's affairs.

"Honey," she said to her friend, "I have an idea. You mustn't see this man again. Every time you see him will make it harder for you to—give him up."

"Sylvia—do you actually think—"

"No, no! I don't think anything. I know he's nothing to you. He's just a friend. You just pity him. I know! I've felt that way before, myself. But it leads to something else. Lou, I'm terribly afraid. You're not like me. I've thought my heart was broken ten times, already. But it never is. I get better. I can forget a man in a month. I've done it. Because they're all rascals. But you, if you ever grow attached to one of them it will be the first and last. I know! You're not like me, Lou. You're really not. You go away from Gorman. I'll meet Mr. Cadigan in your place tonight, when he comes to your house. I'll be waiting outside your window, after dark. I'll meet him there! I'll tell him—"

"What?"

"That you've changed your mind about ever seeing him again and—"

"Not that!"

"Have you gone out of your head, Lou? Dear, do you really want this thing to go on growing and turn into a real love affair? Do you want to have your heart broken by an outlaw, a murderer, a cheap flirt?"

After all, for decision on the spur of the moment, those words were well chosen, and each of them cut Lou Morris like the lash of a whip.

"Go to Newsom and visit your Aunt Margaret. You know she's been begging you to come."

It was vain for Lou to protest. Indeed, her own mind was in such a swirling conflict that she hardly knew what she wanted to say. Sylvia was right; she must be right. And when Sylvia began to urge her to tell her mother quickly that she intended to spend the next day in Newsom, and that the stage was starting in an hour, and that the packing had to be done before it left—Lou was taken off her feet. When the stage left, an hour later, Lou was a passenger. Her last words were still ringing in the ear of Sylvia.

"What you say to him, say it gently, Sylvia. He may be bad. I suppose I'm a fool to think that he isn't. But there's [illegible]

street, followed by a prone column of twisting dust which turned into a funnel, the joint under the rear wheels of the vehicle and the mouth sweeping wide and far behind.

All of this was watched by Sylvia with a cunning look in her eyes and with an expression of immense satisfaction on her face. She had planned this whole maneuver on the spur of the moment, but she felt that she had planned wisely and well, and that victory was even now inclining to her standards.

Now that she had removed Louise the field was open to her, and she could do what she pleased. What she pleased was, in brief, the instant death of this fellow who had dared to lift his eyes in aspiration to her friend.

What she felt about Lou was all, indeed, that one good woman could feel about another. She would have given her life to save that of Lou. And she felt that if ever treachery was justified in this world, it was justified now that she intended to strike this wretched deceiver, this villain of a Cadigan, out of the path of poor Lou. Such was the conviction of Sylvia, and supported by an honest wrath and pride in her actions, though the gravity of the thing that lay before her made her rather pale.

She went straight to find the sheriff. Sheriff Jeff Andrews, after the twenty-four hours which he had spent in the saddle pursuing Cadigan in vain, after that first vain assault in the hotel, had returned, without sleep, to take up the command and organize the long chase from the vantage point of Gorman. He saw the girl at once, and she went straight into the heart of her story.

"Sheriff," she said, "I've come to give you Cadigan!"

The sheriff gave her one wild glance. Then he steadied himself.

"That's a good beginning," he said. "Which pocket have you got him in?"

After that, she told her story swiftly and clearly. There was not much to it, after all. Dan Cadigan had been in that town the night before. He had promised to return again, and unless he heard of the departure of Louise Morris in the meantime, he was fairly sure to come again.

"He's a cool skunk!" said the sheriff, gritting his teeth. "A girl like Florence Curry ain't good enough for him. He's got to look at Louise. Why—I'll—"

"Catch him with your men, or if they miss him—hunt him with your dogs, but if you let him get away from you, sheriff, I'll—I'll never think of you as a man again! I want him torn to pieces!"

The sheriff blinked. He was not accustomed to such talk from ladies, especially young ones.

"That's kind of hard on young Cadigan," he said. "But take him by and large, I dunno that the whelp is worth anything more'n dog food! I'm gunna aim to satisfy you, Miss Bender! What's made you take such a shine to Cadigan?"

She looked hastily around her to make sure that no one was near the door. Then she leaned closer to the sheriff. It was betraying a confidence, but anything that would make the sheriff more determined in his work was worth while.

"Mr. Andrews," she whispered, "he's nearly won Lou. One more seeing of him and she'd—she'd be in love. And you know what that means with a girl like Lou Morris?"

The sheriff knew, or could very accurately guess. His face wrinkled with the pain of that thought, and then his jaw thrust out violently.

"It's gunna be a wild night for Cadigan," he said. "And maybe for the dogs of Bill Symond. You can lay to that, Miss Bender. Might I ask, though, d'you aim to do what you said? D'you aim to be there and meet that Cadigan the way you told Lou Morris?"

"I do!" she said fiercely. "I'm going to be there and meet him just as I said, and the last thing he's to know [illegible]

22

SURROUNDED

The wind swung to the north again before the evening of that day came. The sky from a brilliant noontime darkened toward the evening. The long gray arms of clouds extended southward from the mountainous horizon, thick at their sources, diminishing toward the ends of the columns, like three columns of smoke blown from three funnels of gigantic ships steered for the north pole. All of these signs were given a stronger promise in the mid-afternoon, and before dark the sky was completely overcast. Just in the dusk it began to snow, not with a sudden whirling of the flakes, but only now and again a pale snow flower would flutter like a dying butterfly through the air. When it touched the ground it disappeared at once. When it touched the face of Sylvia Bender as she stood at watch beneath the window of Lou's room, waiting, and savage still with determination, it made her think of many things. It made her think of the chill touch of death. It made her think of the lips of a man.

And Sylvia sighed. She had been without a wooer for nearly a month; and she herself had not been in love for a year. It made her feel a little old, a little stale and behind the times and their fashions.

Poor Sylvia!

When she thought of herself standing there—how prone [illegible]

only one thing to spoil her pleasure, and this was that there was no one to see her there. Alas, if the world could but look in at us at the right times, when the footlights are turned on, and when the features are composed, and when the great lines are well-rehearsed and fairly trembling upon the lips for utterance. If only the world would look at us in such moments! But instead, it prefers to wait and spy at us in the morning, say, when one's coffee is cold and one's cream turns out to be skimmed milk; or at noon—on a hot, nervous day; or on Monday after too much of a week-end; or in the evening when one has failed all day long and even one's temper is at last exhausted. Such are the times when we are seen and known. How many a joyous life is remembered not by its sunny prime, filled with laughter and with wine, but by the gouty evening of dull age!

Something of all this passed in the reflective mind of Sylvia as she waited beneath the window of the room of Louise Morris. It was not all pleasant, to be sure. Sometimes a wave of cold terror swept over her. Sometimes she said to herself: "If he finds me here, he'll simply choke me to death with those terrible hands which were able to handle even big Sam Boswick. One grip would break my neck!"

Alas, how sad a picture when she was borne into the house of Mr. Morris, and how the family would gather around, and how they would sigh as they saw her youth and her pale beauty. Yes, but when one is strangled, one's face turns black, and one's eyes are apt to be a bit bulgy. Besides, even if Lou were sad forever at the thought of this sacrifice upon the altar of friendship, would she be sad enough to make it worth while? Sylvia clutched a revolver which she had brought with her. No, she would be no passive victim. And if Mr. Cadigan were not extremely cautious in his treatment of her, she would send a bullet crashing through his brain!

She had reached this savage humor when a gust of wind beat strongly against her and set her shuddering with the cold. What of men who must roam through such bitter weather as this, whether they will or will not? What of far travelers? Ay, and what of outlaws condemned forever to wander like this, through heat and cold and dry and moist! Such was Cadigan!

When she looked into the sweep of the night it seemed to the girl that Cadigan was like that mountain range to the south, looming huge and ill defined, obscured by night and by the rising storm. Then, as that thought came to her, something slid noiselessly up before her and crouched.

"Barney!" said the voice of a man. "Here, boy!"

The shadow with glimmering eyes drew back, and Cadigan stood before her.

"Why," said he "have you been standin' out here waitin'—why, with this here snow fallin' and your coat all powdered with it and white."

He grew mute with wonder and with emotion. And he stretched out a hand as though to touch her and make sure that this could be true, but the hand fell again, as though he dared not take even so slight a familiarity. It stirred Sylvia with wonder. If this were acting, and acting it must be, how consummate was his skill!

"I didn't expect anything like this," said he. "But maybe they's something you have to tell me—maybe they's something that you've come to tell me to do—is that it?"

What a wealth of hope was in his voice!

"Because," said he, "if I could do even some little thing for you, I'd be the happiest man in the world."

"I have something that needs to be said to you," said the girl, and at her voice he stepped back a pace and drew himself up, while the wolf dog, as though sensing that there was a change and that all was not well, slipped forward again with a snarl as soft as a whisper. But she saw the white of his bare teeth through the night.

[illegible]

his voice which startled the girl. Here, she told herself, could not be acting. But the very thought that she might be wrong maddened her and drove her ahead. There was a death trap set, and Cadigan stood in the center of it. She must be right. She dared not make a mistake here. But the dread that she had erred made her brutal.

"Game," said Sylvia. "Do you think that she was serious when she said that you could keep coming here to see her?"

She saw the head of Cadigan bow.

"Why," she thrilled, "what are you, Dan Cadigan? What are you but a crook, and a man-killer by profession? What are you but a sneak and a thief? And how do you dare to even speak twice to a fine girl like Lou Morris?"

"Why," said the voice of Cadigan, sounding far away, "I dunno that you ain't right. I was wrong all the time. But you see, I wasn't really hopin' nothin'. I was simply hangin' on. If I could see her—that was heaven. If I couldn't see her—that was hell! That's why I tried to come."

It was too real. It shocked Sylvia to the heart. After all, there seemed a very great probability that she had been very, very wrong, and if so, the death of this man was to be laid to her door. She gasped as she thought of it.

"Was that all she said to tell me?" asked Cadigan sadly.

"What else did you expect?" snapped out Sylvia.

"I dunno," said Cadigan slowly. "It seems like I been wrong about mostly everything."

"There *is* one thing more," said the girl, panting as she

spoke. "I'm to tell you, Cadigan—that this is your last night. You're a dead man. They're all around you. That was the only reason that she let you come back. Do you hear me? It'll teach men not to try to make fools of girls after this. It'll help teach them! They're all around you—the best men of Gorman. They're all waiting with their guns. And if their guns should miss you, that's not all—the dogs are waiting for you, Cadigan! Save yourself if you can!"

She ended with a shout of exultation and of terror. What would he do? How would he strike? Or would he send the dog at her? That was what she dreaded most. For the man, she had the revolver ready, but for the dog, one bullet would not do the work unless it were most luckily placed.

She thought that she heard, first, something like a sob. But that might have been a trick of her ears or something in the rising voice of the wind. Afterward she heard Cadigan say in a voice that rang coldly, like iron on iron: "What price did she get for me, then? Does she split with you, or with the sheriff? Or does she get the whole bunch of money herself? Barney!"

And he whirled and was away in a flash. Then she raised her gun and fired, and the answering echo was the shout of a score of men planted around the house of Morris, screening all that side of it with armed warriors of the mountains. Half a dozen guns barked. Their flashes showed the fleeing form of Cadigan.

But escape he certainly could not if he strove to break through that circle of fire.

He saw that at once, and he stopped short. He was wonderfully cool. He could even afford to marvel at himself. After all, it had been as swift as a pencil stroke, striking out a wrong line. He had nourished a last illusion about kindliness and goodness in the world. There was none among men. But one woman—yes, this one gentle exception. Alas, she had sold him like a stray dog, for money!

It would have crushed some men as though a heel had been planted upon them. But Cadigan it stunned, and then it turned him to iron. His mind was functioning more smoothly, more frictionlessly than ever before in all of his days. He gauged the number of the men in that circle by the scattering reports of their guns and by the volume of their shouting. There was no escape that way. A whirl

23

PURSUIT

Past the cowed, crouching form of the girl he darted. He sprang at the window, tore the window itself from its running strips, and dived into the interior. As for the men who were closing in on him, they took no thought for the fact that the girl might still be there. A roaring volley sang about Sylvia and ate into the wall of the house. She was unharmed, but she fled with a scream, and that scream checked the second volley from the repeaters—after the flare of the first one had showed them their targets more clearly. It saved Cadigan, in other words, from certain death. He landed in the middle of the floor of the room. A shadow shot past him—Barney. Across the room he blundered. It seemed a dreadful eternity that he was fumbling for a door, while a strong voice was thundering outside:

"Get around on the other side of the house. Surround the house, or he'll get away. Quick, half of you!"

Other voices made answer. The dog whined in soft terror, as though he, too, knew what terrible danger was closing in around them. Then Cadigan found the door and plucked it open. Down the hall he raced.

They would expect him to issue, perhaps from the rear of the house, to run back among the other buildings and [illegible]

him in the dark. No command to halt, but a gun bellowed and spat red smoke in his very face. He struck for the head, but instead, his fist bit into the throat of the man, and Rickie went down with a strangling gasp. Then the front door.

He had no time to feel for the handle of the door. But, in his full career, he collected his weight and gave it his shoulder. The door sprang from its rotten hinges and let him out, staggering and lunging, into the open night and fairly into the arms of half a dozen hurrying men who were rushing to gain the farther side of the house.

Even had they not been taken by surprise, they were too close to him and in too much confusion to have used their guns without doing more probable damage to themselves than to him. And he tore through them like a bounding boulder through the tangle of brush down a hillside. He split them apart before him, and when they swung and raised their guns, there followed him the swift sliding form of Barney with a snarl so horrible that it made them leap sideways out of his path.

However, though he might have escaped from two rings of danger, there were still others before him. Into the roadway before the little house had galloped on the rush the reserve of picked men which the wily sheriff had so skillfully planted. When his deputy had asked him, before, if he thought that he were planning a battle with an army or with one man, he had said with much conviction that sometimes one man was harder to beat than an army. It was harder to see him, for one thing! However, here were mounted reserves to cut down the fugitive before he was well started. Three men, armed to the teeth, were instructed to parade in front of each side of the house the moment that there was an alarm. And the three in front of the house were certainly prompt to meet the requirements of their duty.

To run away from them was impossible. To turn his back upon them and try to flee in another direction would be, simply, to invite destruction from behind. So he did the one thing which remained. He charged straight at them, with the wolf dog whining savagely at his side, as though imploring him to dart straight away toward the forested slopes of Gorman Pass, where they would be sure of shelter in the woods. How could he understand that the man had not the swift foot of the wolf to carry him on as though on wings?

The three saw him plainly enough. There was neither moon nor stars to help them, and the flurry of a strong wind always makes for bad marksmanship even in the day. But they had the dark form of Cadigan against the white of the house of Morris, and they could not have failed to kill him if they had had a chance at any distance. The trouble was that he was pursued from behind by half a dozen of these men through whom he had just rushed. They dared not fire from behind for fear of hitting the horsemen; and the horsemen dared not fire for fear of striking their companions upon foot.

Their very strength in numbers was paralyzing them. But when Cadigan leaped over the fence—with the huge shadow of Barney vaulting it beside him—they opened fire regardless of consequences, and at the first discharge sent a bullet through the calf of the leg of young Walter Henley!

Three guns had roared before him. Then Cadigan leaped at the central figure of the trio like a wild cat at bay. One hand clutching the mane of the horse helped to swing him up. The other hand, balled into a fist, was a club which struck the rider senseless from the saddle. And Cadigan sat in his place. His left-hand neighbor, with a yell, fired straight at his head. Then Cadigan, closing on him, tore him out of his saddle and hurled him against the road.

There was the strength of an angel or of a devil in Cadigan, now. Make even a weak man desperate and he [illegible]

plunge from the saddle to the ground.

Then he himself was rushing down the road at the full speed of his horse while Barney, with a wild howl, more wolfish than ever, raced ahead.

Fully twenty revolvers and rifles roared behind him. But what was that to Cadigan? He was free and away! In a dozen strides his horse was whipped around the corner of a shed. In a dozen more, two buildings were put between him and the pursuers.

There were other riders shouting behind him, cursing at the top of their lungs, but something told Cadigan that they would not be too reckless in closing upon him.

They swept on into the open beyond the town. Straight down the pass rushed Cadigan. He rounded into the road and still he fled at close to the top speed of his horse. It was no extraordinary animal, this one which he bestrode. It was simply an honest range pony, a sturdy old gelding with a fine head for cutting out, but with no exceptional gifts in the way of foot. No doubt half of the dozen riders who were so closely packed behind him could have overhauled him easily enough. But they did not choose to, and Cadigan smiled grimly to himself as he thought of the reason.

He decided to try them again. Drawing a revolver, he sent a random bullet plunging into the air straight overhead. And then another. At once the pursuers grew dim behind him. If Cadigan felt that this was effective range, apparently they were willing to take his word for it. They dropped back until they were quite out of sight in the dark of the night—only the rumble of their hoofs in the road, and when this had been accomplished, Cadigan turned to the left and headed straight for the northern side of Gorman Pass.

He was in no hurry now. He had a peculiar, almost light-headed feeling that, now that Lou had sold him and now that there was nothing left in life which was really worth the pain of existence, it would be extremely hard for him to throw away that valueless life. In the meantime, let them close in behind him if they dared!

He found a rifle slipped into the holster at the side of this saddle. He drew it forth, knew by its weight that it was a Winchester, and then tried to snapshoot at close range at a tree which he was cantering past.

He could not see the effect of the shot, but he knew with a perfect certainty, a thing which astonished him, that he had struck his target. He knew, as surely as though a line had been drawn from the muzzle of his gun to the trunk of the tree itself. He *could* not miss!

Somewhere among the tales of wild men which float around the camp and the bunk house, he had heard strange stories of men gone wild and desperate in outlawry who were endowed by a destructive providence with the ability to hit their mark, no matter how difficult it might be—quiet men, gentle fellows, men who had never fought—were turned into sure-handed destroyers. What if this thing had come upon him?

And he knew that it had! The thrilling certainty of it grew and grew in him. If others, most unremarkable men, had become terrible through their desperation, what would he become, who had won even the admiration of Uncle Joe Loftus before this change took place in him?

They had run him out, he told himself, without a fault upon his part, and for the sake of what they had done to him, he would destroy them root and branch, if God were willing—root and branch he would destroy every man who took his trail!

That fury lasted in him while he braved the rush of the north wind climbing the slope, but when he dropped down into the hollow beyond, he told himself that it was folly to kill. Many killings simply meant a short existence. To kill was not what was wanted, but to do harm. That was the thing which he would make his god!

He sent the mustang slowly up the slope beyond. And, [illegible]

24

BARNEY, REAR GUARD

Yet he did not fall into a panic of fear. He felt, somehow, a perfect surety that he was reserved for more work, more mischief in the world, or otherwise he could not have gone through the peril at the Morris house that night, by miracle it seemed, as he looked back to it.

He pushed his horse steadily ahead. And there was this advantage in his mount. If it were not fleet of foot, at least the gelding had endurance, and it had, above all, a wise head to pick its way through the darkness and the rough going. There was no longer the sound of horsemen behind him. They had fallen back, doubtless, to let the voices of the dog pack show them through the night like lanterns toward the prey.

Presently, when he reached a stream, shallow and wide, he sent the horse snorting down the current. For a full mile he rode, slowly, the gelding laboring more and more through the wet sands, or reeling with the force of the current. He did not leave the water until the clamor of the hounds showed that they had reached the water's edge. Then he turned again to the north. A more obvious thing would have been to double back on his course. But he was bent on leaving them some sort of a trail puzzle, no matter how simple. There in the darkness, where the hunters would be unable to help the dogs pick up the trail, they [illegible]

It lifted his heart a little—until the thought of Lou came back again and turned his soul to a thing of steel. If she was evil, then all in the world was evil. So much as this was perfectly plain.

He had ridden on, without haste, for a full two hours until, pausing to breathe his horse on a low eminence, he heard a sudden faint jangling sound behind him. The hounds again! In spite of himself, a prickling chill passed down his back.

Then he stirred the weary gelding with his spurs and went on. Now that the dogs had straightened out on his trail, however, they were coming fast. No horse can live against the speed of a good hunting pack, and Cadigan knew it. Neither was he sure where, through the mountains, he could come upon a new mount. In the meantime, he must plod away and hope against hope to make his escape.

But how swiftly they closed behind him! Two deep voices, chiming in close harmony, led the rest. The trail was so hot that they did not need to fall back and wait for the surer guidance of the bloodhounds. Two of the fighters of the pack—two of those gaunt warriors who were wisely kept half starved by Bill Symond to increase their hunting edge and their ferocity, were closing fast behind him.

Twice Barney, growing disturbed, ran ahead of Cadigan and disappeared into the night. Twice he came back again and leaped around the head of the gelding as though wondering at the fatal slowness of the master when speed, full speed, was needed. For this was not the first time that dogs had hunted Barney, and he knew all their dangers!

A third time Barney left him, when the yelling of the pack was growing stronger every moment. But this time it was to dart to the rear with his gliding wolf's stride. Cadigan, wondering, half thinking that the big anmal had lost its senses, and peering back from time to time as he urged the staggering horse ahead, had his explanation at the last. A short, shrill cry of a beast in agony rent the air behind him. Then another wild yell began and trailed away toward the rear, presently lost in the tremendous clamor of the whole pack in the distance.

And then Barney came again and Cadigan did not need sunshine to tell him that the mouth and the white vest of Barney were richly mottled with crimson. He spoke his greeting, and Barney leaped high beside him with a whine of happiness. If this were the game, he was willing to play it, it seemed. He would make the rear guard in this long retreat!

Then, as they topped the next rise, Cadigan saw in the valley beneath him the sight for which his eyes had long been hungry—a ranch house and the widespreading buildings clustering together, surrounded by a spidery thin fencing, in the distance. He could not help a groan of relief, and the poor gelding, as though it realized that relief were ahead of it, raised a tottering gallop as it went down the slope.

But still the dog pack gained with a terrible consistency. Those two deep organ notes were no longer racing in the lead, but others were joined to it. Once more Barney dipped back out of view in the shadow of a hollow and came into sight again on a rise beyond. Over the rise, presently, streaked the form of a racing dog. It met Barney. Only for an instant they closed. Then another death howl filled the air, drowned by the cry of the full pack as it rushed in for vengeance.

Vengeance on what—a smooth-sliding ghost? For yonder was Barney, gliding across the top of the rise, clearly defined against the horizon stars, and after him trailed the entire pack! He had led them astray, and Cadigan, seeing the wisdom and the cunning and the generous courage of that act, felt his heart swell in him. If there was neither generosity nor justice among men, at least he could find [illegible]

[illegible]

coming. Their dog pack had stretched far away to the left; but the horsemen themselves had not made that mistake. They had been near enough to see their target as it fled before them! What a torrent they made! Twenty—thirty hot riders—some half dozen closely knotted together in the lead and the others trailing back into oblivion as they flogged their weary horses along. Here was a fresh mount for Cadigan, but here were fresh mounts for all his pursuers, as well.

If he wanted any great advantage, he must pick the first of the lot—far the finest, for his weight was a crushing impost upon even a stout animal. There was no doubt as to the king of this herd. A big gray shook his crest above the rest, snorting at the sight of the man with the rope. At him went Cadigan. The herd split away on either side, the gray rushed off with the milling throng to the right, and the rope whirred from the hand of Cadigan.

It was a long cast and one made at a swiftly moving target, but just as Cadigan had known that his rifle bullet would find its mark through the darkness, so he knew now by a perfect premonition that he could not fail. No, the rope settled around the head of the gray, and at that touch the trained animal planted its hoofs and slid to a halt. In thirty seconds the saddle was cinched upon its back and its teeth had been pried open to admit the bit. Then, from the secure height of the saddle, rejoicing at the strong barrel of the horse which he felt between his knees, sensing the working muscles even through the flaps of the saddle, he took stock of the pursuers.

They were coming fast, fast down the slope, like water hurtling down a mill race. But still they were not too perilously close—considering that there was no brighter light for shooting than the dull glimmering of the stars. There still remained time for one most necessary maneuver, and Cadigan performed it. It was simple to ride to the bars, jerk them from the gateway, and then with a wave of his hat send the whole caviya scampering out into the open fields toward safety.

Let them catch their mounts in that hundred-acre field when they could. He rushed the gray at the fence, and the big fellow rose and sailed it like a bird. He landed lightly on the farther side and rolled away in his full stride, lightly and strongly, holding his head high, so that the mane fluttered behind his neck, and keeping his little ears pricked, as a horse of high heart should do. This was a horse indeed! And Cadigan laughed through his teeth as he saw the pursuit split into two parts. One group drove straight after him, firing as they came. The others spilled into the field to catch new mounts.

He had divided them, at least, and in the meantime, if they wanted more racing, let the gray give it to them!

There was no need of whip or spur. The good gelding snorted as he felt the rein loosened, and then he gave himself to his work.

A light was kindled in the window of the ranch house as Cadigan shot by like a comet. A door opened and a voice shouted, but how far away was the gray before the noise of the slamming of that door reached him?

For five minutes Cadigan let the fine fellow race over the rolling ground. Then he looked behind him, and the mass of the posse was blurred together in the starlight, losing ground at every stride. And faint and far the dogs were chiming. They had had work, much work this night. But if they would catch Cadigan now, they must move very fast indeed!

Something came canting up behind him. It was Barney, lolling his long red tongue and greeting his master with a deep whine of happiness. He was running as easily as though he had not just worked the legs off the fastest pack of hounds in the mountains. They had been called back from the dog to the trail of the man, at last, but not until the throats of two more of the pack had been torn out by this dreadful fighter. And still he frolicked along as [illegible] even that pace put the staggering posse farther and farther to the rear.

25

THE BANK HOLDUP

The old Cadigan, even that resolute fellow who had come down to Gorman the night before to find Lou Morris and try to tell her that he loved her—even that Cadigan would have been a weary man after such a night's work. But the new Cadigan, who was born in that dreadful moment between the last works of Sylvia and the first bullets from the sheriff's men—that Cadigan rode into the morning light with a whistle on his lips and not a line on his face.

He had treated the gray gently for the past hour, and the big fellow was dancing with readiness to go when they reached the ranch house where Cadigan decided to breakfast. The punchers, in the rose of the morning light, were gathering for breakfast and washing their faces at the pump near the kitchen door, when Cadigan drew rein. There were half a dozen of them, and they looked at the newcomer half sleepily until one of them said: "Ain't that Joe Moore's gray."

"That's Joe Moore's gray or I'm a doggone rabbit," said another, and they all stared.

So Cadigan threw his reins and dismounted. He hitched deliberately at his belt and stretched some of the cramped feeling out of his legs. And yet he was not tired. There was an inexhaustible well of energy in him which had

[illegible]

coolly, "I didn't stop to ask his name. He wasn't on hand to tell me. But if he's a friend of yours, one of you might take his hoss out to the stable and give him a feed of oats—or barley, if you ain't got oats handy."

They only gaped at him. Then a frown walked across their brows. Here were six strong men. Yonder was only one. Here were six strong men, and though they were not wearing guns, what of that? No guns showed on Cadigan, for that matter. But still, he had them. They knew it, and they knew that he was aware of this information. Yet it was not a matter of guns. There was something else—that same thing which had flowed in upon Cadigan the night before, when the trap at the Morris house was revealed to him.

"One of you can trot along with him," he repeated sternly. "You, Buddie, in the red shirt, you can do that little errand for me, I guess. And hurry it up!"

He pointed a forefinger to pick out his man, and the latter started as though it were a gun which had been pointed at him. For a single instant he hesitated, with battle showing dark in his eye. Then without a word he took the reins of the horse and led it toward the nearest barn.

"You can wait till he's ate his oats," said Cadigan. "Then you can bring him back here. I guess I'll be through with my breakfast by that time. All right, boys. I guess we'll go in and chow."

All in the blackest silence they trooped into the dining

room and there they found the rancher, a big young man with a hard face which a pleasant smile made almost handsome, seated at the head of the table. He waved good morning to the boys and smiled on Cadigan.

"Morning, stranger. Set down and make yourself to home."

"Thanks," said Cadigan, and chose a corner chair.

The others took their places. They needed no advice, and on either side of Cadigan a chair was left vacant. This the rancher regarded with some surprise.

"Ain't any of these boys pals of yours?" he asked genially.

"No," said Cadigan. "I just happened along."

"Doggone me, if you didn't put up in the bunk house, you must of been ridin' all night."

"Most of it," said Cadigan.

"Where's Jack?" asked the rancher sharply.

There was no answer.

"Jack wear a red shirt?" asked Cadigan.

"That's him!"

"He seen my hoss was hungry, and he took him along to give him a feed. He'll be back—when the hoss is through eatin'. Mighty thoughtful young chap, that Jack is!"

The rancher stared. Then he pushed back his chair a little, and glared about the table at the sullen faces of his men.

"What in the devil is all this about?" he demanded. "And who might you be, stranger?"

"Me? My name is Cadigan."

Like the snapping of a whip over a team of horses which had gone dull on the road, so every man started. It was a silent breakfast at that ranch.

Not a word was spoken. The whisper of the truth had gone out to the cook, and he brought in the dishes one by one with shaking head and retreated with staring eyes of fear. But Cadigan ate with an excellent appetite, and still with all those men in the hollow of his palm.

The others finished long before him, and finally one pushed back his chair to rise.

"Set right still," said Cadigan genially. "The part of

the country that I was raised up in, they had a rule that it was good manners for everybody to stay at the table till everybody was finished. I dunno about how things are round about here. But I aim to like good manners, partner."

orders. The cook muttered his assent. And still the party remained around the table until the pack was made. Then Cadigan marched the rancher through the door ahead of him.

"In case they was any accidents," said Cadigan, "it might come in handy to have you around to put things right," he added without malice. "But doggone me if this ain't a silent crowd. No singin'—no fun! You lead a mighty dull life out here!"

"Cadigan," said the rancher sternly, "this sort of talk ain't doin' you no good. You can't play your hand agin' everybody. I give you that bit of advice—along with the bacon."

To his amazement, Cadigan stretched forth his hand with a smile. And the rancher shook it, wondering as he did so what chance he would have if he threw himself suddenly upon the desperado. Around him, his men were stirring uneasily, ready to rush in the moment their chief made a move to attack. And still the big fellow did not act. There was something in the steel grip of Cadigan that told him his own life, as least, would be torn out of his body if he stirred. There was something, too, in the eyes of Cadigan, which told the rancher that he would be giving up his life in vain. It would take a greater power than that which was assembled here to quell the outlaw.

So he watched Cadigan's horse being led back; he watched the pack made snug behind the saddle; he watched Cadigan deliberately turn his back and then vault into the saddle. Nothing could have been plainer—this man was playing with danger—deliberately inviting death. And when such invitations are extended, all thinking men will hesitate. They hesitated now, while he waved good morrow to them and jogged away without so much as a backward glance. When he had gone a little distance, they saw a huge form, larger than the largest wolf that they had ever put eyes on, slip from a patch of shrubbery and fall in at the side of the stranger.

"I can get him now with a long shot!" murmured one of the punchers hastily to the chief.

"Leave him be," said the rancher frankly. "If you missed—darned if I don't think he'd find a way to come back here and kill us all! He's bad medicine, that boy is!"

So Cadigan rode on, filled with a grim joy. He had found himself, and what he had found was a treasure of unspeakable strength. He cast about, deliberately, for what he might need. In the first place, though his rifle was good, it might be better. He could use a gun of the newest and the lightest and strongest make. He must have one. His saddle, too, was not of the best and must be "exchanged." As for the gray horse, it might not be the finest in the mountains, but it was very good, and he had an affection for Joe Moore's gray.

An hour later, in distant view of the very ranch house where he had breakfasted, he unsaddled, rolled himself in a blanket, and went to sleep at the edge of a thicket where there was ample fodder for the gray. He slept until mid-afternoon. Then he wakened and resumed his journey.

An hour or so later he sighted a town. It was more than a mere village. There must be fifteen hundred or two thousand in this prosperous community and in such a place there must be a bank. And where there was a bank, he could find the cash that he needed. For he had decided against plundering right and left. To be sure, society owed him what he needed to live on, according to his estimation. But that, he could not feel, justified him in robbing Joe Moore, who might not be able to afford the loss of his horse. A little bank robbery would be better.

He rode into the town with no attempt at disguise. In the central business block he tethered the gray at a rack and found the bank at once, by the steel bars which showed behind its plate-glass windows. It was a very small building, but its wealth might be enormous. Such an institution as this was, might finance an immense sweep of cow range,

the canvas sack and pushed it out through the window to Cadigan.

All this while the alarm bell buzzed throughout the building. Cadigan heard it and knew what it meant.

"If you was a year older or a bit less foolish lookin'," said Cadigan without emotion, "I'd blow your head off for startin' that alarm."

Then he ran for the front door of the bank. Three guns barked behind him at the same instant. One bullet sliced through his coat across the shoulders. The others missed—narrowly. For the standard of marksmanship was high in that bank. It had been tested before!

By the time he reached his horse they were dropping on their knees at the door of the bank and firing with rifles, but all they did was to nip the end of the ear of the gray and send it down the street like a racer, swerving a little from side to side to confuse those who fired from behind, while Cadigan flattened himself in the saddle. Then he dipped into a by-street and the noise of the firing died behind him. Ten minutes later he was outside of the town, had been rejoined by Barney, and was looking back over his shoulder at a swarm of mounted men, riding furiously. The town of Cormack was not accustomed to accepting such insults.

For three days that posse hung doggedly on his trail. But at last, when he was sitting the saddle on his fourth "borrowed" remount, he shook them off and journeyed on in freedom.

It was for the moment only. Never once did he get out of his head the saying of Uncle Joe Loftus, that sooner or later he would be cornered, and when he was cornered, he must die. For two things only he prayed daily. One was that he could get at Bill Lancaster before his own end came, and the other was that he might die with both of the guns of Uncle Joe Loftus kicking against the heels of his hands.

FACE TO FACE WITH RICKIE

Within the next two weeks he broke the hearts of three sheriffs who tried to catch him. Within that time, also, the official description of the outlaw had changed. He was no longer presented in print to incipient fortune hunters as a sleek-faced young man, but as one twenty-two years old, or thereabouts, but looking nearer to thirty—a thin face, a straight mouth, and a remarkable straight-looking eye. That was how the literary artists who worked in the name of the law tried to tell about the change which had come over the flesh of Cadigan to match the change which had come over his spirit on that night in Gorman which now seemed so long ago. All these days he had been leading a life filled with a strange happiness, for the newness of his discovered self had not yet worn off. The marks of the minting were still a curious patterning for Cadigan, and every day he thought of himself as of a stranger.

Then he met Cal Hotchkiss. He had trekked far north into a land of snow. Horses were left behind him. Snowshoes served him instead. And, on a day, across the waste of thick, soft snow, he saw a stranger coming toward him. Cadigan waited. Indeed, he always waited for danger, whenever that was possible, for he had a deep-rooted hatred of turning his back upon men or upon events. He saw a burly fellow, at last, striding across the snow with a step which told of much practice with the shoes. When he came near he hailed Cadigan with much warmth.

"You're Cadigan," he said.

"I'm Cadigan," said the latter, working his fingers inside the mittens—in case those fingers should be needed on the butt of a gun a moment later.

"I'm Cal Hotchkiss," said the stranger. "Maybe you've heard tell about me?"

"I've heard," said Cadigan without warmth.

The other, however, was not discouraged. "I been workin' on your trail for ten days," he said. "I aim to put up a business proposition to you, Cadigan. I need a partner. And you're the kind to throw in with me."

Cadigan smiled. The fame of Cal Hotchkiss was bruited East and West and North and South through the entire country. There was nothing from train robbery to bank robbery which could not be laid at the door of Hotchkiss in quantity. He was one of those universal villains who refuse to form habits of crime. Anything was good enough for Hotchkiss, the newer the scheme, the better. He had sold stock for oil wells that were not, and he had exploited towns which did not exist. Hence the smile of Cadigan, and the other, seeing it, nodded and grinned. They knew him as of old.

"I know," said he. "You figger this is another bunco game. But I'm talkin' straight. Two heads are better than one, and two hands are a darned sight better. Will you talk business, Cadigan?"

Cadigan shook his head.

"Have you ever heard that I double crossed a partner, son?"

"It ain't that. I like my life the way I live it—alone, Hotchkiss."

And that was the end. There was more talk, but he could not be persuaded.

"Tell me, then," said big Hotchkiss in the end, "what you're drivin' at, wanderin' around the way you do? Hell-raisin' for the sake of the hell-raisin'?"

"That," said Cadigan, "is about it."

"Well," said Hotchkiss, "if you got anything on your mind that needs doin', I advise you to start for it pretty [illegible]

It was terribly cold. The horse was already half dead with exposure, and Cadigan was numb from head to foot when, as he sat eating in haste, he heard a dull click, as of a knife cutting through soft food and striking a plate. He looked up to see a man standing in the night not twenty paces away with a revolver leveled at his head.

He had grown careless in his vigils, for ordinarily Barney took scrupulously good care that nothing living should approach the camp, but on this evening, Barney was foraging somewhere far off. It was only for the return of the great dog that he waited before journeying south again. So he had come to the very elbow of death.

He thought of all this in the tenth part of a second while he looked at the leveled gun and whipped out his own. His bullet brought the other crashing down, and Cadigan rose and stumbled toward him through the snows. When he jerked the man on his back, he found himself staring down into the face of Richard Morris, and Richard Morris glared back at him.

"Finish me," said Morris. "Finish me, but don't leave me here to die slow—by the cold."

"Where did that slug drill you?" asked Cadigan thoughtfully.

"Through the leg."

"The thigh, eh?"

"Yes."

"It's the doggone cold," apologized Cadigan. "I never

missed as bad as that before. I aimed to kill you the first shot, Rickie."

"Thanks," said Rickie through his teeth, as a spasm of pain seized upon him. "It was the cold that saved your rotten life, too, Cadigan. It must of thickened up the oil in my gun. Doggoned if I know how it happened to misfire."

"Well," said Cadigan, "lemme have a look."

"Darn the lookin'. It's easy to see that I can't get away from here by myself. Finish me up, Cadigan. I ain't afraid to look at your gun, but I'm awful afraid of layin' here till I freeze. You'd put a dog out of misery, Cadigan!"

Cadigan sat down on an ice-sheeted rock and deliberately lighted a cigarette.

"A dog," said he, "is one thing, and a gent like you is a whole lot different. What's brought *you* on my trail, Rickie? Ain't your family done me harm enough already? Ain't I done enough for you by not turnin' back there to Gorman and wipin' out the whole lot of you? Will you answer me that?"

The boy grinned in agony at Cadigan and said not a word.

"Did you hear me ask you a question?" said Cadigan.

"I heard you ask it. I ain't talkin' no more," said Rickie.

"We'll see if you can't be sort of persuaded." He raised his boot above the wounded leg as though to stamp on it. "Will you talk, Morris?"

The boy groaned. "What a devil you are, Cadigan. I've heard tell something about you. I didn't know that a man could turn into a thing like what you are—into a snake like you. Do what you want to with me. I'm through talkin' with you."

"It was the money that brung you along, I guess," said Cadigan, lowering his foot without executing his threat, and puffing deliberately at his smoke. "How much have they got on me now? Since they blamed that Butte City Bank robbery on me, they've boosted it to fifteen thousand pretty near—ain't they?"

"I dunno," said Rickie. "I dunno about that!"

Here Cadigan started and peered more intently down at his captive.

"You don't know about that?"

"You heard me say it the first time, Cadigan, if you won't finish me—reach me my own gun!"

[illegible]

Cadigan?"

"You," said Cadigan, "that've sent me out here and put fifteen thousand on my head—you that've come up here and tried to shoot me in the back—now you talk about a skunk? Rickie, ain't you got no sense of humor?"

"Not," said Richard, "about rats—and Cadigans!"

But Cadigan only smiled. He had heard desperate men curse him to his face before. And now he rather enjoyed this thing. But in the first place, there was the matter of the wound. He had never from the first glance intended that the boy should die here in the snow. Not from the first glance, for that glance had showed him in the wounded boy's face a shadow of what was Lou Morris—a mere hint of something in the eyes and the brow that reminded him of the girl.

It was not a peculiarly critical wound. It was only the cold and the difficulty of getting Rickie to a place of secure shelter that made it endanger his life. The cold had at least had the effect of checking the bleeding. Now Cadigan bandaged it well. Then he cast about him for a means of transport. There, above timber line, they could not stay.

"Which way," he asked, "to the nearest town?"

"Meanin', I s'pose," sneered Rickie, "that you'd take me there if you knowed?"

"You fool!" growled out Cadigan with a black devil leaping into his face. "Which way toward the town?"

The pain, or the threat in the face of Cadigan, subdued

Rickie suddenly. "Straight west," he said. "Straight as a string."

Then he collapsed with a groan.

Cadigan let him lie where he had fallen and set about making his pack secure on the back of the horse—a very strange pack, for he discarded the saddle and cut the girths away from it. Then, with girths and lariat and with tarpaulin and one blanket he made what might serve as a pack saddle. In the other blanket he wrapped young Rickie Morris and, raising him to the back of the horse, strapped him as securely as possible in place. Barney having returned from his hunt, they turned due west and began their march.

27

CADIGAN LEARNS THE TRUTH

They crossed the slippery region of above timber line safely, with Cadigan partly leading the horse and partly holding and steadying Rickie in his place. It was not until they reached the comparative safety of the timber below that a mishap came, and then it was a dire one. For the poor horse slipped a forehoof into a crevice of the rocks and fell with a shock that brought a cry of torment from young Morris and that snapped the bone of the horse's foreleg squarely in two below the knee.

There was nothing for it but to put the poor animal out of pain. And Cadigan did it and came back to Richard Morris with a gray, twisted face.

"That's one thing more agin' you and your kind," he said darkly. "Now, how far is it to that town?"

"God knows!" groaned Richard. "I don't. And—Cadigan, what d'you aim to do with me?"

Over that problem Cadigan dared not pause to consider. Cold had already turned the face of Richard blue, and an extra five minutes of exposure might prove the turning point between life and death. There was nothing for it but to try his best, though he felt when he tried the bulk of Richard that it was a game he was sure to lose.

But he raised Richard, draped the arms of the boy over his shoulders, and strode forward toward the town.

The first half mile was easy enough, but after that, the thing became an agony. There were a hundred and ninety pounds of bulk to young Morris, and in addition, some twelve pounds of heavy clothing, to say nothing of the blanket which Cadigan had knotted around the body of the wounded man. And the ground under foot was either deep in snow or else slippery and sticky with snow beneath the trees.

He fell into a red haze. He became exhausted; then his limbs grew numb, but still he fought on, pausing more and more often to lower his burden, rest a moment, and then go on.

"There's no chance," said Richard at last, in one of these halts. "God knows that I appreciate what you're tryin' to do. But there's no chance, Cadigan. Leave me here, and gimme one of your guns before you go on."

"If I was to do that," said Cadigan, "would you tell me one thing?"

"Anything in the world, partner."

"What made you so dead set on runnin' me down—if it wasn't the price on me, Rickie?"

The other set his teeth. "Anything but that," he said heavily. "I'm darned if I can tell you, Cadigan. It—was just something that I figgered I had to do, because nobody else seemed able. It wasn't for me. I didn't want no money. I didn't want no glory. If I'd done it, I never would of told a soul on earth that I'd managed it. It wasn't for my sake, Cadigan."

"Whose sake, then?"

"Old-timer, I can't tell you."

"It was Lou," said Cadigan slowly. "She got to hate me that much. She wouldn't let you rest until you'd done your best to get rid of me. Was that it?"

"Hate you? Her?" gasped out Richard Morris. "Why, man alive—the reason that I started—"

"Well?"

"Cadigan, why shouldn't I tell you? I got maybe not

more'n another hour left to me. I can't die leavin' that lie in your mind. Why, Cadigan, the reason why I started on your trail is because she loves you, man!"

[illegible]

you say!"

"I swear to God I do, man!"

Cadigan dropped back again to the ground and sat cross legged, his head between his hands, trying to think, but finding that every effort of his mind left him in a deeper muddle.

"I don't make no head or tail to it," he said. "She lays a trap for me, and she baits it. She brings me in to die, Rickie, and she has the sheriff's gents posted around to see that I don't get away—why, man, what kind of—love —might you be callin' that?"

Rickie was staring at him, bewildered again. "You ain't heard the truth about that?"

"Ay, Rickie. I heard the truth about that. The bullets singin' past my head told me the truth about that!"

"But it wasn't what you thought. It wasn't Lou that done it."

"Did I dream it, then?"

"It was Sylvia Bender. She meant it all well. She figgered what the rest of us figgered—what I thought—what everybody thought—that you was no good, Cadigan. But Lou, she seen something else. She must of guessed what I been findin' in you tonight, with you bustin' your heart to help a gent that's tried to shoot you in the back. Why, Cadigan, she loved you all the time!"

Cadigan drew a great breath, but still his head would not clear; there was a great wave of joy beginning to rise in him, but he fought it back. There was a torment of wild hopes taking hold on him, but he shook them away.

"It was when Sylvia found that out—the way that Lou felt about you, that she figgered something had to be done. She found out, too, that you was coming back to see Lou the next night. She got Lou to go away. That was right after you'd held up the Newsom stage."

"I never held up the Newsom stage."

"You never did? You didn't hold it up and kiss the Curry girl, and tell 'em your name as you rode off?"

"Me? Never!"

"Lord, Cadigan, that was what turned Lou agin' you that day. That was what persuaded her to let Sylvia meet you that night in place of her and give you your walking papers. But then when she got Lou out of the way, she went ahead and planned the rest of it. She told the sheriff that you was coming—and when he had things fixed, she met you."

"Wait!" cried Cadigan. "I can't stand it, Rickie. It's chokin' me. It wasn't Lou?"

"Why, Cadigan, she's been eatin' out her heart for you all this time!"

Then Cadigan rose like a giant and raised his burden again. There was no weakness in his limbs, no dizziness in his brain, no fumbling of his feet as he strode forward, and at the very next break in the trees, he saw the lights of the village glimmering before him.

28

DANNY GETS A SURPRISE

Red and then black lightning was shooting before the eyes of Cadigan when he reached for the doorknob, and then slumped forward on his face. When he recovered, he was lying in the middle of the floor with a wild waterfall raging in his brain and a great fever burning him.

"How's Morris," he asked a woman who leaned above him.

"He's comin' through," she said. "How you feelin'?"

"I'll be movin' along," said Cadigan, and promptly fainted again.

Once more his eyes opened. His eyes were dark and cold with a fresh-water compress which had been laid across him, and there was the pungent burning of whiskey in his throat.

"Are you better?" asked the voice of the woman.

"I'm comin' on fine. Only—a little sleepy," said Cadigan.

He fell away again and heard the woman's voice say out of the great distance: "Poor devil!"

Of what could that be said? Certainly not of the terrible

Cadigan! Then he smiled a little to himself, faintly and this time it was more of a sleep than a collapse.

Out of it he wakened finally and found himself staring up at the cracks of a very clean, white ceiling. He stirred and moved a leg—behold, he was wonderfully weak. He lifted his arm, and before his eyes there arose a thin, pale hand.

"Why, darn my eyes," said Cadigan, and propped himself up in the bed.

Straight across the room, between him and the window, sat an elderly woman with a vaguely familiar face.

"I'm sorry," said Cadigan.

"You'd best be lyin' down," said she, smiling.

"Me?" said Cadigan. "Why should I be lyin' down?" Then he added, before she could answer: "How long have I been here?"

"About nine days, come tomorrow," said the other.

Cadigan twisted his head around quickly. At the door sat a man of the range with a sawed-off shotgun across his knees. That was the answer to his unspoken question.

"I see they're takin' care of me," he said, and grinned at the guard.

"We're doin' our best," said the other good-naturedly, and grinned back.

"When I'm strung up," said Cadigan, "I hope to heaven that it's in a town like this. What might the name of this here town be if—"

He stopped speaking, for the woman at the window had dropped her sewing and was sitting erect, her hands folded in her lap, her face twisted with horror and with pity.

"Why," said Cadigan, "doggone me if I ain't sorry that I said that. I didn't mean to cut you up, lady!"

She shook her head and managed a smile; but almost at once she rose and hurried from the room.

"The devil!" said Cadigan to the guard. "I wouldn't hurt her for a lot. I ain't to think that she's been takin' care of me for a spell."

"Ever since you come here—till she got spelled a few days ago. She wouldn't let nobody help to take care of you except—"

"Except what?" said Cadigan.

The other grinned back at him and shook his head. "Talkin' ain't always safe," said he. "I guess you'll get on for a while without knowin'."

Cadigan glared at him in much irritation. However,

"Shut up," said Cadigan. "Listen to that bird singin'."

Through the opened window the sound poured in.

"It reminds me," he began, and then changed his mind. "Well," said he, "I guess I dunno exactly what it reminds me of. But I'm mighty glad to hear that doggone bird. Seems like I heard it before—while I was sleepin'."

"I guess you heard a bird, all right," said the guard with his usual provoking innuendo.

"The devil," said Cadigan. "What might you be drivin' at now?"

"Nothin'," said the guard as before, and shifted his sawed-off shotgun importantly upon his knees.

"D'you aim to be a fightin' man with that there gun?" asked Cardigan scornfully.

It was impossible to anger this man, however. He merely grinned back more broadly than ever.

"I'm a fightin' man enough to guard you while you're in bed, old son!"

Cadigan rolled over on his back with a snort of disgust. Also this talk had made him oddly weak, and he wanted to close his eyes and shut away the light. There he lay, very feeble, his heart racing, and thoughts driving rapidly through his mind. Nine days of delirium!

"Gimme a mirror, will you?" said Cadigan at last. "I want to see how I look in whiskers."

"Sure," said the guard amiably. "Anything I can do to make you comfortable, you just let me know about it, will you?" He strolled across the room and brought Cadigan a small hand mirror.

"Hey!" said the sick man. "The way you talk, a gent would think that you was my nurse and not my guard."

"Why," said the other with his maddening smile, "in a way of speakin' I'm both of them two things!"

Cadigan growled savagely at him and then raised the mirror. What he saw was not recognizable as himself, certainly. That starved, hollow-cheeked stranger with the somber eyes was certainly not Cadigan—not the old Cadigan of the sleepy days—not even the new Cadigan of the name of terror. He put down the mirror in disgust.

"I dunno what's happened to me," said Cadigan aloud.

The chuckling voice of the guard made answer: "You'll soon find out, you lucky son of a gun!"

Cadigan propped himself upon his elbows and glared at the man with the gun.

"Darn your miserable heart!" said Cadigan. "What might you be meanin' by that? Are you tryin' to will me with curiosity? Is that it, maybe?"

"Wait a minute, old son," said the guard softly, raising his hand. "Listen to that, will you?"

A door had closed quietly somewhere in the distance. Hurried, light footfalls swept toward the room.

"I reckon the old lady has told her that you was awake," said the guard.

"Reckon she told who?" gasped out Cadigan.

The guard shrugged his shoulders. "Give you time," said he, "and you'll see for yourself, if—"

Here he stopped short, for the footfalls were rapidly nearing the door and now she swished into view and stood there with fear in her wide eyes, but with a smile of excited happiness on her lips. It was Lou, more wonderful than the dream which had filled his delirium, a sad-faced Lou, grown pale and serious, but now wonderfully lighted by her smile.

She ran to him and dropped on her knees beside the bed. "Danny, Danny, Danny!" said she. "I thought you'd never wake up! I thought—no difference what I thought—you're back, now, and we'll never let you go away again. You mustn't sit up—lie back—Danny. Lie still. What'd the doctor say if he knew that you were sitting up? Now do as I tell you."

"I dunno what he'd say," said Cadigan. "And I don't care. All that I want to do is to—"

[illegible]

"Oh, Danny, I'll have to go away if my coming makes you get so excited!"

"I'll make the guard lock the door—doggone me if the guard ain't gone. How's that, Lou?"

Lou had turned a bright red. "I don't know," said she with great indifference. "I suppose that he had something to do outside—and—"

"Lou," said Cadigan, "is it true?"

"Is what true?" said she, a darker red than ever.

"That—you know what!"

"I don't. I don't at all. And—I think I hear some one calling me, Danny."

His thin hand caught her dress and held it, but though there was no strength at all in his finger tips, there was enough to detain the girl. She slipped again to her knees.

"Hush, Danny!" she said. "Will you stop tormentin' me?"

Some one had called happiness golden. Now Cadigan knew that it was the right name. Miles and miles of beautiful golden light—such was the happiness which flowed in upon the soul.

"I'll stop tormentin' you," said Cadigan gravely, "but some day you'll tell me—"

"What?" asked Lou, and then she corrected herself in a terror of haste.

"No, no!" she said. "Don't answer that!"

Cadigan looked up to the ceiling and smiled. All great things must be silent. So was the exultation of Cadigan.

29

A BARGAIN IS STRUCK

The sheriff was fond of saying that he was a mild man, and, indeed, there was hardly a person in the world who would have said otherwise of honest Jefferson Andrews, with the exception of those who had actually seen him fight. But on this morning, the sheriff, at the sight of a girl, changed color and attempted to flee, damning softly and steadily as he did so. He went straight for the back door of the hotel and ran down the steps, only to find himself confronted by her as he turned the corner, at the very moment when he congratulated himself that he had escaped.

He managed to drag off his hat, and then he strode along, saying: "Sorry I got to be movin' along. I hope I ain't interruptin' no business that you was to talk over with me, Miss Morris?"

"You go right along," said Lou, falling in at his side and keeping her place with a marvelously long, long step. "My business takes me the same way that yours takes you."

Here the sheriff allowed a muffled exclamation to escape from him. He halted and stared down at the girl. "What might you be wantin' out of me this mornin'?" said he.

"Just a chance for a little talk," said Lou.

"Amount of time that folks spend on talkin' would pretty nigh serve to keep the old world spinnin' along."

[illegible]

[illegible] wolf!" roared the sheriff. "By rights, that brute had ought to be shot. It's done more murders than any two men in the world. And if Bill Symond was ever to meet up with it—after what it done to his pack—I guess that he'd finish Barney!"

"Oh, no," said the girl, "not while Cadigan is left alive, I guess he wouldn't! I—I took Barney into Dan's room this morning. You would have cried if you'd seen the way they carried on with each other! You'd have cried, sheriff. *I* did!"

The sheriff snorted, but Lou was wiping an actual tear from her eye at the mere memory.

"Maybe I would," he said. "I reckon that a lot of folks would feel the same way—seein' a outlaw and a wolf carryin' on that way and a respectable girl out of a respectable home standin' by and weepin' over them!" The sheriff turned a bright purple and glared at Lou as though he would sweep her from the earth.

At this, she lifted her chin so that the sunlight played and quivered along the curve of her throat, and she laughed at him, softly, deliciously. The sheriff sighed.

"There ain't no way of handling some young folks," he meditated. "They's a doggone lot of rambunctiousness goin' on around these here parts! I'll tell a man!"

"Another thing has happened," said Lou.

"I dunno that I got any more time to talk," said the sheriff. "I got an important engagement downtown with a—"

"We decided that we'd get married," said Lou.
"Damnation!" roared the sheriff. "Are the two of you both crazy and all crazy?"
"I suppose we are," sighed Lou.
"Maybe," said the sheriff with a sort of malicious dryness, "you aim to wait till he finishes his term in prison?"
"Will they really send him to prison?" asked Lou.
The sheriff raised his trembling hands to the blue sky. "Now, God forgive my soul!" said he. "He's a gent that's robbed stages—"
"He never did, though. He didn't, sheriff."
"Trains—"
"Not a one!"
"What makes you think so?"
"He told me so," said Lou blandly.
The good sheriff was staggered. "If he told you to jump in a river, I suppose you'd do it," he said gloomily.
"I suppose I would," said Lou, "if it would make him any happier—bless him!"
"A bank robber, too," said the sheriff.
"After they drove him out into the wilderness—after they'd shut him out. What could he do?"
"Bah," said the sheriff. "I can't talk to you no more, Lou. It makes me plumb sick!"
"I'm sorry," said she meekly.
"Here you are, fit for—" he swallowed. "And throwin' yourself away on a—" he swallowed again.
"I don't quite make out what you said," said Lou.
"You know mighty well," said the sheriff. "A bank robber—a doggone gun-fightin', man-killin'—"
"Did he ever kill even a single weeny man in his whole life?" cried Lou angrily.
"Well," growled out the sheriff, "talkin' so much and claimin' such a lot for him, you got to be right once in a while. But he's shot up enough gents to serve for a couple of murders. Nothin' but luck kept him from it!"
"Straight shooting saved him!" said the girl. "He never shot to kill, and you know it, Jeff Andrews!"
When a woman calls a man by his full name, it is time for him to beware. The sheriff stared at the flushed face of the girl and sighed.

"Aw, Lou," said he, melting, "what in the world can I do for you and the boy? Puttin' people in jail is my job —not gettin' 'em out. But what can I do?"

"Dear Uncle Jeff!" said the girl [illegible]

[illegible] being reelected if he lets them send to prison a poor boy who was railroaded into trouble—blamed for things he never did—made into an outlaw—and then when the *sheriffs* can't capture him for all their men and all their guns and all their *smartness*—he just comes in and gives himself up trying to save the life of another man, a man who'd tried to—to—*murder* him!"

The sheriff sighed. "How long are you gunna carry on?" he asked. "How long d'you want me to listen?"

"Until you promise with all your heart to try with all your weight to get Danny pardoned!"

"It can't be done!"

"Then set him free!"

"Lou what are you askin' of me?"

"What God would bless you for doing, Uncle Jeff!"

The sheriff could stand no more. He turned on his heel and strode hastily away, jerking his hat lower over his eyes and cursing roundly at every step which he took.

Behind him, the girl drew a long breath of relief, then brushed back her hair and dabbed a tear out of her eyes.

"Thank heavens," said she, "that's done, and done right. Dear old silly Jeff Andrews. He's such a baby!"

The sheriff, in the meantime, thinking of guns and powder and death, strode on down the street until he came to the house where Cadigan was half guest, half prisoner. And all the way he was hailed with queries of one sort.

"How's the boy, sheriff?"

"How's the prisoner comin'?"

"I hear that Cadigan is comin' round."

"You take good care of young Dan, sheriff. We got a need for men like that!"

A fortnight since, and every one of them would have risked death for the sake of the glory of destroying the great outlaw for the sake of the reward which was upon his head. But now all was changed. What fool has said that happiness can be earned by evil deeds? Here, in a trice, after half the crimes in the calendar had been charged against Cadigan, he was freed from blame, purified from all his past life, made into a spotless hero by a single act of generous self-devotion.

There was never a day passed that flowers or fruit or food was not sent in to good Widow Carney for the use of the two invalids. She could have fed ten men with what was sent to him.

As for the widow herself, after much debate it was decided that the reward for the capture of Cadigan must be given to her. At least, she had been the only person near when Cadigan reeled through her front door and collapsed along her floor. To whom else could the reward be paid? And manifestly it must be paid to some one.

When they broached the subject to Mrs. Carney they were met with a rude rebuff: "Reward for what?" she said.

"For taking Cadigan."

"Why should there be any reward?"

"Why, figgerin' on all the crimes of the—"

"How dare you!" cried Mrs. Carney. "Run along with you and don't bother me no more with no such talk. Reward for the crimes of poor Danny! What sort of rewards will *he* get for the good things he's done?"

Nevertheless the reward was paid to her. Because, as has been said, there was no one else to whom it *could* be paid. Thereat she sent back the check for fifteen thousand and some hundreds of dollars. She sent it addressed to the governor of the State, and she included with the check a free contribution of some of her own private thoughts and of some of the emotions which passed through her when she thought of men who dared to offer money for the life of such a "dear good lad as Danny Cadigan that ain't no trouble even when he's sick!"

The governor bit his lip when he received this communication. Then he obeyed his better angel and caused the letter to be published. It was exquisite meat for the [illegible]

All of these reflections were passing through the brain of the sheriff. After all, he wanted to see Cadigan free and safe. So did every one else. But how could it legally be done?

He stamped his way into the house and into the bedroom of Cadigan. "I've seen the girl you sent to me," said he.

"Me? I ain't sent anybody. If Lou has been naggin' you ag'in—"

"Shut up," said the sheriff, "and lemme have a chance to talk. I never seen the like of how you young folks don't give your elders no chances to say nothin'! What I want to know, I say, is what can be managed to make this here legal. Suppose I was to turn you loose?"

"Sheriff, I can't ask that of you."

"Shut up, Cadigan. Hear me talk. Suppose you was to go free lancin' around the country and try to find out the gents who robbed the P. & S. O. train? Some gents that know might talk to you where they wouldn't ever talk to me! You understand?"

"Are you serious?"

"Serious as the devil! You're near well enough to be sent to jail. If we do anything, we got to do it now."

"It'd be betrayin' your trust," said Cadigan thoughtfully.

"All I would be doing, son, would be to let you out on parole. You give me your word to come back when I get ready to send for you!"

30

CADIGAN SEEKS CAL HOTCHKISS

Three nights later, when a warm, steady rain had blown up out of the south, they sent the guard on an errand, and Cadigan simply walked out of the house, mounted a horse, kissed Lou Morris as she wept for joy and sorrow foolishly commingled, and then galloped away into the night.

The next day, he read a newspaper which told in much detail how he had escaped, in spite of the great precautions of Sheriff Andrews, who in a solemn statement vowed that he would make it his sole business to recapture the escaped reprobate. The paper stated, also, that the sheriff's effort to raise a posse had not met with any great success. There were few volunteers; all the enthusiasm for the pursuit and capture of Cadigan was dissipated in a trice, except, as the paper editorially stated, for the "head hunters" who would still be scouring the mountains to find their man and their fortune at the same time. The paper went on with further editorial comment upon those who were raising questions as to the diligence with which the sheriff had guarded the escaped prisoner. The record of Andrews was too long, said the editor, to be blackened by casual talk, and inquiries into his motives and his behavior were little short of foolish.

All of this was comforting to Cadigan, but his work still [illegible]

till in the West. But how to even find Hotchkiss?

He decided to get in touch at once with that wireless system which nets the continent—the trails of the "hobos" who wander back and forth from State to State, braving danger, facing a thousand dangers because their horror of death is less than their horror of work.

He headed for the first town with a "jungle," and found it located under the railroad bridge, shrouded with a thicket of tall trees, with the great iron girders and pillars of the bridge arching overhead. It was bitter winter on the ridges of the mountains, but in this sheltered valley the weather was far milder, and out of the forest which swept up and down the valley, the tramps could collect a seasonable store of wood for their fires. He found half a dozen men shivering about a blaze when he entered the jungle, half a dozen men with faces black with grime, and with unshaven beards, gloomy, savage fellows. But his name was all he needed with which to unlock their hearts.

They admitted him to their circle; they examined him with almost shy glances. They ventured, at last, upon questioning.

"What was the game, after all, draggin' that kid into town and puttin' your head into a rope?" they queried.

To have confessed the truth would have been to convince them that he was lying, or else to win their scorn and mockery at once.

"It was a long shot that I was playin'," said Cadigan mysteriously.

"Did it pan out?"

"Sort of half way," said he.

They nodded, satisfied.

"You fixed the sheriff, I guess?"

"I ain't talkin' about that," said Cadigan, but he permitted himself to wink at them. And they were delighted. This was enough to base a story upon.

He waited for another half hour or more before he answered frankly, in response to another hint: "I'm on the trail of Cal Hotchkiss. D'you boys know where he's at?"

"Are you after him?" they asked him.

"I want to join up with Cal," said Cadigan.

Over this they mulled for some time, but the apparent frankness of Cadigan was quite convincing. So they told him. A hobo has little to do other than pick up tidings in one place and carry them to another. Their minds are constant depositories of news; and the movements of those who are great in the criminal world are constantly and accurately recorded. So they told Cadigan where he could find his man. And he started on the fifty-mile journey at once.

It led him over the first high ridge of the mountains, then twisting down the valley which lay beyond, and finally it took him to a deserted ruin of a ranch house. There was no Cal Hotchkiss there. But Cadigan camped and waited patiently. The second night something wakened him from his sleep, and he sat up in his blankets to see Hotchkiss sitting in the moonlight, his lined, ugly face turned dreamy with the content of a cigarette.

"You've showed up at last?" said Cal Hotchkiss.

"I thought I'd better drop around."

"Well," said Hotchkiss, "you've gone and got holy since I seen you last. What in the devil was in your mind, savin' that young rat instead of shootin' his head off?"

"I had a hunch of my own. It didn't quite work, though."

"You thought that they'd give you a pardon and a brass medal, maybe. Well, they didn't."

"That's it."

"So you've come back to old Cal to see what's hoppin'?"

"I have."

"All right, son. Speak up. I ain't needin' you so bad

as I was. But I still could use a good man now and then. What d'you want out of me?"

"The names of them that held up the P. & S. O. train [illegible]

[illegible]

"What'll you pay?"

"Money?"

"Of course not. I mean—they's a young gent that has been trailin' me for some time. He's a poison mean snake of a gent that's been blackmailin' me. I want to get rid of him. What d'you say, Cadigan?"

"Is he a crook?"

"Worse'n a snake!"

"I'll try him," said Cadigan.

"I mean—kill him, Danny!"

"Why not—if he's a skunk?"

"It's Hugh Furness."

That was enough, indeed. All men knew the rat face of Hugh Furness. All men knew that his life was filled with horrible evil. He still lived partly because of his ferretlike ferocity and cunning, partly because men shunned him like an unclean thing. He was dangerous as a rattler; he was secret as a coyote. Cadigan shuddered as he thought of the creature.

"Furness has something on me," said the big man. "It's something that I can't let out. So he's been bleedin' me white with what he knows for a long time. Now I got to get rid of him. I'm tired of being milked! Cadigan, will you take the job?"

"I will. Where do I find him?"

"At old Burnett's place. You know that?"

"Where Sim Burnett killed his uncle last year?"

"That's it. They're friends of Furness."

Cadigan rose.

"If you kill him—how'll you know that I'll have the news you want when you come back, Cadigan?"

"I'll take a chance. Your word is good enough for me, Cal."

It was after midnight; the night was iced with a wind off the snows; and the whole conference which determined Cadigan had not lasted five minutes. But his mind was made up, his direction was given, and he could not wait. In another five minutes his horse was heading down the wind, trembling with the cold, and Barney was striding at his side.

31

CAL FINDS AN HONEST MAN

He had passed the Sim Burnett place only once before, but it had an expression like a human face. It could not be forgotten. It lay between a marsh and a bald hill, a little house from which the sun had peeled the paint long ago, staggering, so it seemed, into the lee of the hill for shelter, but receiving none. The house swayed all to one side, like a living thing shrinking from a blow, or a coward fleeing.

There was not a stick or a shrub or a tree near the house. Some said it was simply the improvidence of wicked old Sim Burnett, who went out with his ax and always turned into firewood the nearest thing. Others said that the clearance had been made with a purpose and a policy in mind, because Sim Burnett loved to see his prospective visitors afar off, though he never rushed out and fell upon their necks; neither did he kill the fatted calf for them, except that ancient partner in his crimes—Hugh Furness.

At any rate, as Cadigan approached close to the house he felt, even before he saw it, a great loathing as for some unclean, infectious disease, and when he saw the house, a moment later, in coming through the hills the loathing increased to a shudder of disgust. Yet it was not so loathsome as during the summer. The marsh had been a rotten mass of decayed foliage and green-scummed waters; now its ulcerous filth was skinned over with a flat face of ice from which dead reeds thrust up like hairs in the stubble of an unshaved beard.

The house was muffled to the eyes against the winds of winter. In the rear, the old barn had received one shock too many after an adventurous life, and it had dropped inward—all the northern portion being involved in a common ruin. The southern part still stood, though threatening to fall every day, and part of the northern half had been cleared away. No doubt it was used for firewood, and lazy Sim Burnett looked upon the collapse of his barn largely as though it were a godsend—a veritable windfall!

Cadigan rode up to the front of the house in a fierce humor. The nearer he came the more disgraceful appeared the condition of the place. The windows were stopped with sides of boxes nailed crooked across them, or where there were a few panes of glass remaining, the other broken places had been filled with wadded old clothes. He felt very much like touching a match to the house and sending the inmates forth in this fashion rather than venturing into its filth.

But he dismounted, threw the reins, and watched Barney lie down across the end of them, for it was the practice of the dog to guard the horse of the master and never leave it while Cadigan was away. It was a safer protection than a man with a ready gun.

With his retreat thus protected, Cadigan stepped to the front door and knocked. Once and again he repeated the summons, but the door was not opened. At length he stepped back and, looking up, he made sure again that his first observation had not been wrong—certainly there was a wisp of smoke climbing into the gray winter sky from the chimney which thrust up like a strong fist through the broken back of the building.

He went back and beat on the door with the butt of his revolver until suddenly the door was cast open and Hugh

Furness himself came into view, his face convulsed with maddened malice.

"You tramp!" he yelled. "Are you tearing the house down?"

[illegible]

to the icy edge of the wind. He was very tall. He would have stood a full three or four inches above six feet if he had erected himself to his proper stature, but instead of that, he walked perpetually stooped, as though the weight of his long, narrow head were too great for his spine. He was the color of yellow mud—greasy, yellow mud. A scant growth of long-haired mustache decorated his upper lip like wires. There were only two young things about him—these were the infinitely cunning little black eyes, sharp and active as the eyes of a rat, and the long, bony hands. Those eyes were young to see, and those hands were young and strong to seize and to tear. It seemed a marvel that God could have put so horrible a caricature of a man upon the earth.

"You're from Hotchkiss," said the monster, swinging his big right hand for the first time away from the revolver at his hip. "Well, what's he got to say? How much did he send? Or did he send the whole thing?"

"I'm from Hotchkiss," said Cadigan, "but he didn't give me no money for you."

"He didn't?" The ratty little eyes glittered at Cadigan, jumping from point to point, insolently, judging him, and at last coming back to the level, scornful stare of the younger man.

"He didn't," repeated Cadigan.

"Who might you be, young man?"

"I," said Cadigan, "am the rat killer."

It required only a moment for the truth to penetrate

the brain of Hugh Furness. Then he swayed with rage, and his lips twisted up from long, yellow teeth.

"Why, kid," said he, "are you drunk?" And he writhed his long fingers around the butt of his revolver.

"Good!" said Cadigan. "I thought maybe you wouldn't fight. Pull your gat!"

"You're tired livin', maybe?" asked the other.

"Maybe that's it. The world is tired of you, too, Furness. You're gunna die. Not the way you murdered young Ollie Peters—while he was sleepin'. But you're gunna die."

"That's right," said Furness. "I knifed Peters. He wriggled like a stuck pig while he was dyin'. But what I aim to do to you—you won't wriggle none, kid! I'll do that much for you—I'll finish you quick as—" And he interrupted his words with the jerk of his hand.

His gun cleared the holster, the muzzle tipped up—then the flicker of light at the right hip of Cadigan exploded and Cadigan stepped to one side as Furness, dropping his gun, reeled forward clutching at the air with both hands, and fell upon his face.

There Cadigan left him. Sim Burnett, when he returned, could attend to the burial. He whipped into the saddle again and spurred away as from the presence of a nightmare, and so back across the countryside, riding steadily. That night he made a dreary camp in the timber; the next day he was at the ruined old farmhouse waiting for Cal Hotchkiss.

Cal was not on time. For three long and weary days Cadigan waited. Then the big man returned suddenly in the middle of a cold, bright morning, and strode into the house. He sat down by the stove, where Cadigan had kindled a fire, and warmed his hands.

"I heard about it," said Hotchkiss. "I hope you told him that you came from me?"

"I told him that."

He waited. "About the P. & S. O.," said the outlaw. "It happened so long ago that I had to stir around more'n I had expected to. But finally I got on the trail. I met up with a gent that used to know Sam Boswick—you know—the Boswick that Duds Malone killed two weeks ago?"

He added: “Why, that was the Boswick that you met up with, once—the strong man!”

Cadigan nodded.

“Boswick told this pal of his all about it. Him and [illegible]

“Back in Gorman. He’s a big man in the town, now, it seems. Look here, Cadigan, did you ever do anything that wasn’t right square before they accused you of that robbery and run you out?”

“No.”

Hotchkiss nodded: “That’s it,” he said. “That’s what makes the difference between you and—the rest of us. This here Rickie Morris—it wasn’t no game—you was just doin’ your best to save the young fool?”

“That was it.”

Hotchkiss sighed, and then he stretched forth his hand. “I been waiting twenty year,” he said, “to shake hands with an honest man. I guess I’ve found him!”

32

LANCASTER SETTLES DOWN

Spring came to Gorman on the heels of the Chinook wind. It melted a foot of hard snow and ice in twenty-four hours, revealed the black earth, and choked the rivers with yellow waters and with thunder. Then followed open-faced, sunny days. The air was languid; the flowers began to come singly, and then in waves of delicate colors over the hills, making them like sunset in midday. And all of Gorman put off its heavy coats and slickers, and stretched its arms, and came forth to look at one another and forget the hard times and the wrinkled faces of winter. Hard words were forgotten; new-born enmities died again; and old friendships were refreshed. Voices grew softer, eyes grew more open.

It was a perilous time for young hearts. And what heart so susceptible as that of Sylvia Bender?

All winter she had lain under a pall of doubt and suspicion of herself. What she had done for her friend, Louise Morris, had been done with none but the very purest and the highest motives in the world. But yet a doubt had crept in. It was not that Lou had ever so much as reproached her, but that was only because, as Sylvia knew, there was too deep an agony in the spirit of her friend to permit words to express what she felt.

So she saw first little and then nothing of Lou. They [illegible]

There was the fresh strain of learning about that strange affair between young Rickie and the outlawed Cadigan. There were the tidings of the journey of Lou to the north to nurse the sick man. There was the story of the escape of Cadigan, which men were most willing to attribute to the willful negligence of the sheriff, and finally there was the return of Rickie, limping, very pale, and with a defiant look about his eyes, together with his sister.

Something had happened to Lou. Every one noticed it from the first. She went about singing all day. And yet what it was that had made her happy no one could tell. It was common news that she loved Cadigan. It was common news that he loved her. But here was her lover an outlaw on the face of the earth—truly a strange situation to gladden the heart of a young girl!

Sylvia could not stand it. She went straight to Lou, at last, and asked her point-blank: "What in the world has happened to you, Lou?"

The answer was as frank as though it were the most ordinary thing in the world. "He's told me he loves me, Sylvia, and I've told him!"

It was a cause for contentment which Sylvia could hardly understand. "But—dear—with poor Danny away—and hunted—aren't you dreadfully afraid for his sake?"

At this, Louise Morris looked away and shook her head. "I didn't know," said she. "I suppose he's in great danger, but nothing seems to matter very much as long as we understand."

"Will you and he ever forgive me?" asked Sylvia.

"Why, Sylvia, I'd forgotten all about it. And so has Dan, I know."

Sometimes it is not so pleasant to be forgiven, because, as in the case of Lou, it seemed very largely synonymous with being forgotten, and on that day which should have been a day of reconciliation, the gap between them grew greater than ever. Lou, sad, had been one thing, and a most appealing thing; but Lou, happy, was quite another. However mysterious the riches of her happiness, it certainly was hers, and Sylvia, rather desperate and lonely, cast about her for some resources of her own.

At the very first dance she found them in the person of a tall gentleman with a remarkably handsome face, a pair of fine, dark eyes, a deep, strong voice, a wealth of natural grace, and a reputation out of which the fame of a dozen ordinary men could have been carved. Yet he was hardly thirty!

It was Bill Lancaster. He rarely went to dances, and he told Sylvia so. He rarely called on girls, and he told Sylvia so. He rarely wasted time in idle chat, and he confessed this to Sylvia as they sat in the parlor of the Bender house. And they had reached this state of things when the spring rushed over the mountains on the heels of the Chinook and took them both by storm.

It was the time of year when mute young men have their only good fortune with ladies, because ladies hardly have to be wooed in the spring. Their imaginations, which may have slept all winter as securely as any grizzly in a cave, waken and look hungrily about. Almost any man makes a pretty fair hero in May; and on certain starry-faced nights in the latter weeks of April a veritable Indian would have attractions.

At the end of a week Lancaster proposed; and though Sylvia ached to accept him, she had wit enough to refuse. That was all that was needed to really fix the hook in Lancaster. He was bewildered by such a rejection, and after that moment he haunted her daily. He put his pride in his pocket and allowed the entire world to see that he was lost in deep love. And when, two weeks later, Sylvia thought it was not inexpedient to say "Yes," Lancaster swore that he was the happiest man in the world, and he believed it.

However, he was a prize not to be taken too lightly, and [illegible]

assorted trio to act as partners. She did not feel that a man so grave and middle-aged as Ches Morgan or so young and thoughtless as Duds Malone, quite belonged in the company of her future husband. But, according to Lancaster, they had been through more together than she could ever guess, and they had tried one another so thoroughly that he, Bill Lancaster, had not the slightest doubt that fortune would always smile upon their endeavors.

Fortune had indeed smiled upon Bill and his "partners." In his position as a favored deputy sheriff under Jeff Andrews, suspicion could not so much as glance toward the big man, and he used that broad shield of the law as a defense under which he and his two associates operated. Pooling all of their resources after the train robbery, they had close to twenty thousand dollars among them. After their operations of the winter were completed, that total, in spite of much free spending which had delighted the hearts of the storekeepers of Gorman and Newsom, had risen to the very handsome figure of fifty thousand. It was with this capital that they bought the old McKenzie ranch over the hills and refitted the house. One wing was to be reserved for Sylvia and Bill. The other wing was to serve as general headquarters for the hands and for Ches and Duds.

It was only three nights before the wedding that Sylvia returned from the ranch after a last careful inspection of the house and its furnishings. It was a little rougher than she might have liked, but, as they declared to one another, "they could build together"—they needed no flying start!

Now they jogged smartly homeward, with the team of fine bays whipping the buckboard smartly over the road, and as they went, they outlined the future.

"And you, dear Bill," said she, "will never, never again do any—fighting?"

Lancaster grinned on the most removed side of his mouth. "Ne'er a bit," said he, and winked at the hilltops far away. Once they had turned the actual corner of the marriage, he could do as he pleased, but in the meantime, it would be very wise not to take too many chances with a high-spirited girl. Such was the diplomacy of Bill Lancaster.

"And I've heard about Duds—is he really a very dangerous man, Bill?"

"Him? Oh, I'll handle him, all right. He hates to stay put. Most likely he'll spend half of his nights away from the house. Comin' and goin' all the time—never can tell when. That's Duds. Queer about that!"

He might as well prepare her for some of the things which were to come in the future. So he added briskly: "Ches is the same way. They're a pair, that way."

"As old a man as Mr. Morgan?"

"Well, he ain't so old. It's just a habit, you see. They like to get movin' after the sun goes down, like city folks."

She nodded, but she was only half convinced that this was well. And, in the meantime, she heard the rapid tattoo of hoofs pounding in the road behind them.

"There's some one coming, Bill," she warned him.

"Well, there's plenty of room for him to pass."

"But he's not trying to pass. He's staying just the same distance behind us all the time."

Lancaster looked around with a start. He could see, riding on a strong, big horse not far behind them, a horseman who was in fact keeping an equal distance behind them always. Whether Lancaster sped up the horses or slowed them, the stranger kept at the same distance, and as Lancaster scowled in wonder at this conduct, he saw a thing which explained it to him perfectly. For among the shadows at the side of the road he saw a swiftly skulking figure of a dog as big as a wolf, or bigger, indeed, than any wolf which Lancaster had ever seen in all of his life. He saw and he understood. It was Cadigan who galloped behind him, and the coming of Cadigan could mean only

33

A BAD MISS FOR LANCASTER

At the same instant they turned around a sharp elbow bend of the road, and they were screened for an instant from the view of the pursuer. In that instant Lancaster acted for the love of his life.

He slapped the reins into the hands of the astonished girl and, crying, "Drive on straight for town!" he leaped out of the buckboard with such violence that the whole rig lurched to the side and Sylvia screamed with terror. That cry made the horses bolt. She was busy for the next minute in trying to steady them and straighten them out from their rapid gait; when she looked back again, the view of Lancaster was lost to her, and with terror in her heart, she let the horses flee on toward the town.

Lancaster, in the meantime, crouched at the side of the road in the shrubbery with both his guns in his hands, squinting down one of them for a snapshot the instant the pursuing horseman swung into view, and when he came, he fired. It was a bad miss for Lancaster, for the target was close and big, but the nerves of Lancaster had just received such a shock as they had never had before except in a certain bunk house months before.

Before he could follow that first shot with a second, [illegible]

to pursue rashly through such a place would have been madness.

Cadigan simply remounted his frightened horse and called Barney back from the pursuit with a shrill whistle. And Barney came, skulking and savage. Even his brute mind seemed to comprehend that a cowardly attack had just been made upon his master and upon himself, but he was forced to follow meekly while Cadigan turned his horse and journeyed on up the road.

In the meantime, Sylvia Bender reached Gorman in a panic state, but yet with enough to know that it might well be better not to tell the truth. She had heard the sound of guns behind her. It might mean that big Lancaster was dead, by this time, but whatever she guessed at, she knew that he had leaped from the buckboard like a fear-stricken and desperate man, and that he had by no means played the bold part of the hero whom she was to marry before the week was out.

Indeed, Sylvia thought more about that problem than she did about the actual fate of her lover. She hitched the team in front of the hotel. Then she hurried to her father's house and walked anxiously up and down through the garden. A whole hour—two hours; and then, through the thick of the night came a looming form—Lancaster!

He seemed so big, so formidable, that instead of a cry of joy at seeing him alive, Sylvia merely wondered what could have possessed him to flee from any man—from any single man!

So she greeted him in silence, standing with her hands clasped together at her breast. And Lancaster stood above her, plainly in a black humor.

"Well," he said, "what are you thinkin', Sylvia?"

She had never heard that tone from him before, or from any other man, for that matter.

"I can't think," said she truthfully enough. "I can only wonder—who was he?"

"A devil out of hell!" snarled out Lancaster.

"But—Bill, you aren't afraid of him—not really?"

"Afraid?" said Bill hoarsely. "Of him? No, nor of no man! But it's the dog that runs with him. You can handle a man, but you can't handle that devil of a wolf dog, Barney!"

"Then it's Cadigan!" cried the girl. "He's come back—to see Lou!"

"He's come back to do a murder if he gets a chance," said Lancaster. "But he ain't goin' to get the chance. I'll have the town up and after him pretty quick. Only—"

"I'll never stop thinking of his riding behind us like that—without a word. It'll haunt me, Bill! But—what is there between the two of you? Why does he hate you?"

"Because I been helpin' sheriff Jeff Andrews to catch him."

"Do you think that's all?"

"What else could it be?"

"How can you use such a tone to me, dear?"

"I'm not usin' no sort of tone. What I want to know is this, and I want to know it right pronto: How many folks have you told already about—what happened up the road? Tell me that!"

There was such an almost snarling note of challenge in his voice that she started, and his manner stung her into some sharpness in her retort.

"About what, Bill?"

"About—you know!" he seemed unable to make the words come.

"Do you mean about how you ran away?"

His oath was only half stifled. "What sort of talk is that, Sylvia? What d'you mean by it? Besides, it ain't true.

I didn't run away, but with my back to him there in the buckboard, what chance did I have?"

She did not answer. Sometimes silence is the most effec-

[illegible]

What could he say? What was there that could be invented? For all he knew, the buckboard might not have been out of sight at the time when he had rushed blindly through the shrubbery. Even now his clothes were torn to rags by that flight, and his face was whipped and stinging from the small branches which had thrashed across his skin.

"I had to get away from the dog," said Lancaster in a half audible grumble.

She had only been guessing wildly, before—not even guessing. She had not actually dreamed that he had fled. She had thought of him standing face to face with the enemy when she heard the shots. But now his confession struck her like a hand in the face.

"You *did* run from him!" she gasped out.

He saw that he had been tricked and trapped, and his big hands doubled into fists, as though he would strike her.

"What chance has a man got agin' *two* devils like Cadigan and his dog?"

"I thought you've always said that Cadigan is overrated? That he isn't such a terrible fighter?"

"Him? Terrible enough to of killed Hugh Furness."

"Did he do that?"

"That's the news that's travelin' around."

"Oh, Bill," cried Sylvia, "go find him and face him—and beat him! Or I'll never be happy again!"

He thought of a dozen things to say, but none of them

were worth uttering. So he turned upon his heel and left her.

It was all well enough to talk of finding and facing Cadigan. All well enough, except for those who had actually tried it. And Lancaster was one of the number. He went, instead, straight to the sheriff.

"I've got news," said he.

"When is the wedding?" asked Andrews.

"Cadigan is driftin' around."

"What!"

"Cadigan, I said."

The sheriff cursed softly.

"Now," said Lancaster, "between you and me, sheriff, we know that some folks ain't none too pleased about the way that you been handlin' this case of Cadigan. They's some that go far enough to say that you and Cadigan are sort of friendly. Mind you, I ain't one of 'em, maybe. But I say that unless you turn out the boys and make a try for him, you ain't got a chance at the next election. What d'you say, Andrews?"

There was nothing for Andrews to say except: "Where the devil can we hunt for him—and at night?"

"Try my ranch house. That's my guess."

"Why?"

"Him and me ain't never been too friendly. He's got murder in his mind, that young gent has. You can lay to that. And I feel it in my bones."

"Where did you see him?"

"On the road."

"You didn't stop to ask him no questions?" asked the sheriff, grinning.

The big man scowled and, leaning closer, he laid a heavy hand upon the shoulder of the other.

"Listen to me," he said. "It's right enough for kids and girls and fools to talk about fightin' anything that comes into the way of a gent, if he's got enough courage. But they's some things that nobody would do if he's got any sense. Nobody would try to fight poison if he could keep from it—and nobody would try to fight Cadigan! That's the short of it, and it ain't to be repeated. I guess you understand me, Andrews!"

Unquestionably Andrews understood. In fact, he felt exactly that way about it himself. And he began, reluctantly, to assemble his men. He took only six, As for a [illegible] Culigan had showed before that numbers were [illegible]

34

A GREAT STORY WRITTEN

Instinct had made Lancaster guess well the destination of Cadigan. He had gone straight back up the road to the ranch house of Malone, Morgan & Co., and tethering his horse at the edge of the woods, he left Barney to guard it and went down to the house itself.

He cast a circle about it first, made sure that there was only a light in the kitchen, and in the room in front of it, and then came down to investigate further. Through the window of the dining room he saw Malone and Morgan finishing their supper, and there he waited until Morgan rose, lighted a cigarette, and waved good night. He left the house at once, and the patter of the hoofs of his horse began down the road.

It was all the better, in the eyes of Cadigan. One man would serve his purpose as well as two, and would be accordingly much easier to handle. He waited until the noise of the horse was gone; until he saw Malone settled in a chair by the table with the soiled dishes pushed back to give him elbow room, and with a magazine resting upon his knees. Then he went to the front door, opened it softly, pulled off his boots, and stole down the black of the hallway.

He reached the door of the dining room, and as he did so, he heard a sudden scraping as of a chair pushed back. [illegible]

[illegible] ing enemy, might be all the more unprepared for a noisy rush.

With that, Cadigan jerked open the door and leaped into the room. He could see Malone plainly, outlined against the window at the farther end of the room, and more than that, he noted the glimmer of a pair of guns in his hands. He might have shot the man at once, but a bullet might kill, and the death of Malone was not what Cadigan wanted.

He leaped to the side as the guns of Malone sounded; their flash showed Cadigan a low chair at hand. He caught it up, whirled with it as the guns of Malone roared again in the dark, spitting out two sharp little tongues of red fire, and then hurled it straight at Duds.

There was a crash and Malone went back against the wall with a groan. When Cadigan reached him, he lay in a crumpled heap. There was no hurry now. So Cadigan lighted the lamp which had just been blown out, and he picked up the loose body by the nape of the neck. There was a slight cut across the forehead of the other, and a large swelling was forming on the back of his head. Otherwise he was quite uninjured, and, indeed, as Cadigan shoved him into a chair the eyes of Duds blinked open again.

He stared at Cadigan with gaping mouth for a moment before recognition came into his eyes. Then his face went white.

"Cadigan!" he whispered.

"You don't aim to be pleased to see me, Duds?" said Cadigan.

The latter moistened his dry lips and made no answer. "If you're broke," he said at last, "I'm pleased to give you a stake, partner." He added hastily: "Anything I got, in fact!"

Cadigan grinned. He was thinking of another picture—a long train grinding to a halt—the frightened passengers tumbling forth and standing in a line—the cruel wit of the masked men as they passed up and down that line, emptying pockets. That was one picture. This was the reverse of it. And it pleased him immensely.

"It ain't money that I've come lookin' for," said Cadigan genially. "It's only for a bit of a talk, Duds."

"Talk?" muttered Malone, rolling his eyes wildly as he tried to penetrate to the bottom of any hint that might lie behind these words. "Sure," he added, "a gent gets mighty lonely—but—" Instinctively he raised his hand to his cut forehead.

"They's times," said Cadigan, grinning, "when a gent has got to introduce himself sort of quick—before somebody gets to work with guns. Maybe you'll savvy, old son?"

"Sure," said Malone, smiling faintly in turn. "Maybe you're lookin' for news about something, Cadigan. Is that it?"

"Right," said Cadigan.

"Well," said Duds, "I'm free to say, old-timer, that I ain't never wished you nothin' but luck. You could write that down and sign it, and it wouldn't be nothin' wrong! What can I open to you about?"

"A little party that you boys had a little while back."

The teeth of Duds clicked. "We've had our times," he said cautiously. "Who's it that you mean?"

"You, Ches Morgan, and Sam Boswick. Lancaster was in for part of it, I guess."

Malone turned from pale to yellow. "I dunno what you're aimin' at," said he.

"You do, though. I mean the thing that they run me out of town for. I mean what they outlawed me for and tried to shoot me up for, and followed me and hounded me, and turned me wrong for. I mean the thing that you and Lancaster and the rest of 'em let ride on my back, hopin' that it'd kill me and get 'em off your trail!" He leaned forward as he spoke, driving the words home, and Malone winced and shrank in his chair, staring

[illegible]

and who you had to fix before the job was finished. I want all of them things, old-timer. You understand? And you're gunna write 'em!"

Malone set his jaw hard. "I'll see myself in purgatory first!" he exclaimed.

Dark blood flowed into the face of Cadigan, and receding, it left him pale.

"Listen to me, Malone," he said. "Maybe you dunno what a true word it is that you've just said. Maybe you dunno that you *would* go to purgatory if you didn't talk. And you'd get a part taste of it right here on earth before you headed down. Duds, I'm gunna have that yarn."

"You'd do murder for it, then?"

"Murder? Killin' rats ain't murder. It's good work for the town. Why, Malone, I got a hoss outside. I'd see ten gents like you die before I seen him get so much as a scratch. That's what value I put on you. But what you can tell for me—that's different. They had nothin' on me before that robbery. Gimme a chance to clear that up, and no jury can convict for the rest of the hell raisin' that I done. It ain't in nacher to convict me for what I was drove to do. It means a clean name for me—it means a chance to marry a girl that's waitin' for me. Why, Malone, to get that story out of you, I'd feed you into that stove, yonder, inch by inch. The devil, man, I'd enjoy doin' it!"

He rose as he spoke and advanced his set face closer to Malone. And Duds was convinced. He was turned a little sick, very weak, and quite determined that he would live another day if mere talk could save him—or mere writing.

"After all," he said, "you've had a rotten deal. Lemme have some paper. They's a stack of it over in that drawer. Lancaster, he seen to that. Gimme the paper, and I'll write out the yarn."

He sat down presently, gritted his teeth, and began a painful scrawl. But as he worked, with Cadigan walking back and forth through the room with a noiseless stride, enthusiasm for the narrative took hold upon him. The scenes began to come back vividly and more vividly upon his mind. Presently he was lighting one cigarette after another in hot haste, and the story was unreeling itself across his pages as fast as he could dash off the words. The beginning of the plan was there—the faces of the men—the very weather in which they rode—the names of the horses—the description of the pass in the throat of which they had stopped the big train.

Only once he paused and looked up. "This'll make my name the bunk with every gent that's ever knowed me," said he gloomily. "It'll make me look like a skunk givin' away my partners in the deal!"

"Maybe," said Cadigan. "But the minute you finish it, you go free. A mighty lot better to live a new life in Australia than to die deader'n a door nail in the mountains, ain't it?"

Duds Malone had to agree. And when he looked into the stern eye of Cadigan, it was astonishingly easy to visualize cold death putting its chilly hand upon him.

So the great story of the P. & S. O. robbery was written. It became famous afterward. It became famous while Duds Malone was tearing south for the Mexican border. In the meantime, Cadigan did not need to look over the shoulder of the author to tell that he was writing the truth and nothing but the truth. There was manifest earnestness written upon the perspiring brow of Duds, and there was eager haste in the fingers which ground the pencil across the paper, breaking point after point.

"Will our friend, Ches Morgan, be droppin' in on us mostly any time, now?" asked Cadigan.

"They ain't no chance of that," said the writer, hurrying on his work.

Then, just as he finished the task and sat back in his chair, something stirred in the blackness of the open [illegible]

35

AT THE FOOT OF GORMAN PASS

Except in the hands of a few famous men, it is possible to play tag with a revolver and escape with life and limb. Because, except in books, or where some genius with pistols is concerned, revolvers are more apt to gouge out the walls and plow furrows in the ceiling and splinter the floor than to drive a bullet straight at its target. The wrist, even an iron one, is at the best an unsteady support. But where a rifle is concerned, the matter is entirely different.

Even an idiot of the purest dye knows that one must not crack jokes at the expense of a rifle. Its long barrel must be handled with both arms, and when it is so handled, even a dolt can do astonishing work with it. Cadigan was in line with two steady muzzles, and he merely drew a small breath and glanced at the farther end of the room. There was the doorway, but even now it opened, and Cadigan found himself looking down the throats of new guns, with the faces of the sheriff and of Bill Lancaster behind them.

No doubt they expected to see him bolt for freedom even

when such a break meant the most certain death. But they were grievously disappointed. He merely raised his hands above his head and said to Malone, softly: "It ain't my danger. It's yours. Leave that paper where it lies. Or

[illegible]

thousand dollars, gents. Don't let it slide through your fingers, old-timers. Hey, Hank, you step in behind him—Jerry, come in on the other side—and keep your hands up, Cadigan, or I'll blow you to the devil. Hear me?" His wild exultation made his voice break and rise high up the scale.

"I ain't aimin' to make no foolish break," said Cadigan very mildly. "All that I want, partner, is a chance to let the sheriff see this here little letter that Duds left behind him." He was mastered, now, with men holding him in biting grips on either side.

"What letter!" cried Lancaster, starting violently. "Lemme see that—"

"Sheriff!" called Cadigan. "Get that writin'—don't let Lancaster have it, or he'll heave it into the fire—"

Lancaster's reach was long and his move was fast, but the sheriff was nearer to the table, and he scooped up the narrative a secure interval before the big hand of Lancaster swept toward the spot.

He picked it up, and the first words he read were:

"This here is the true story of how Morgan and Boswick and me, with Lancaster helping, robbed the P. & S. O. It begun with—"

The sheriff paused to read no more than was revealed to him by that first glance.

"Look here!" clamored Lancaster. "I claim to get what my partner Malone left behind him. It might be some sort of a business secret that ain't fit for other folks to—"

"You're right, Lancaster," said Cadigan. "It's a business secret."

"You," snarled out Lancaster, "shut your face. It ain't your time to yap, Cadigan."

"Why," said Cadigan, "I was only goin' to say that this here business that Malone was writin' about—it had to do with the railroadin' business, Lancaster. I guess some folks will be kind of surprised to hear that you ever was interested in it, eh?"

It was a stunning stroke to Lancaster. In his fury he balled his fist and raised it against Cadigan, but the fat little sheriff stepped in between and slid the long, cold nose of a Colt into the pit of the big man's stomach.

"It ain't no use," said he. "I don't aim to stand for no rarin' and tearin', Lancaster. I think we've landed the right gent at last. Lancaster, you low-down hound, it was you and the rest of 'em that done the P. & S. O. trick. And you let 'em hound Cadigan pretty nigh to death for it. Ain't that the fact?"

"This here is a plot—" yelled Lancaster.

"Wait a minute," said the sheriff, snapping the handcuffs neatly into place with a practiced hand. "You keep your breath till a judge gets through with you. You may need to do a pile of talkin' then, old-timer."

It was all so sudden a reversal, that half of the men present could not make out what was happening. But they did know that Bill Lancaster collapsed suddenly into a chair and sat with head bowed upon his breast as though the fountain of his strength had been dried up at its source.

But as they rode back toward the town of Gorman, the truth came out and there were hard words for Bill Lancaster every yard of the return journey—hard words for Bill Lancaster and warm-hearted congratulations for Cadigan.

It would be well to show villainy properly rewarded and relate that Bill Lancaster went to prison for a long term. As a matter of fact, he did not. Luck served the rascal to the end. He could say, fairly, that he had never been beaten in a gun fight in his entire life, and that was the literal truth. As for the battle from which he had run away, that could be set down to diplomacy.

But after he had been sentenced, Lancaster broke from jail and disappeared somewhere toward the South. After- [illegible]

[illegible] been done.

Sam Boswick had already paid his penalty. But Duds had escaped over the southern boundary of the country, and at his heels rode wise old Ches Morgan, and was never heard of again.

Justice, it might be said, had failed. But its smaller failure here was counterbalanced, in the eyes of some people, by its great victory in another direction. For Cadigan, in spite of that short, wild career of his, was never brought before the bar of justice. Even the bank from which he had stolen eight thousands, contented itself with that portion of its money which he could restore to it.

But Cadigan and Lou, though they began their life together with a very small cash basis indeed, felt that money had little to do with the life that lay ahead of them. They settled at the foot of Gorman Pass, where the hills spread wide and low, and where the grass grew thick and rich. And in the perfect fullness of their happiness there was only one shadow, which consisted of two old revolvers, laid away in a drawer and wrapped in oilcloth. But in that household, they were never mentioned; and no one in all the valley ever dreamed of asking why Cadigan never wore a gun.